"I want you to go to bed…now!"

"Bed…" Georgia's mobile features betrayed her, shock crimsoning her already pink face.

As Piers saw the expression in her eyes, and realized just what she was thinking, he cursed silently under his breath.

"You're shivering, you might have caught a chill." As he spoke, he involuntarily moved closer to her.

"No!" As she lifted her hand from her body to ward him off she inadvertently stepped back onto the hem of her big towel.

Only loosely secured around her body, the towel began to unwrap itself.

Immediately, Georgia made a despairing grab for it and just as immediately, Piers launched himself across the gap that separated them, every instinct propelling him to do the gentlemanly thing and protect her modesty. The towel, though, and perhaps fate, too, had other ideas so that all Georgia's hands encountered was empty air whilst Piers's were unexpectedly and explosively filled with warm, silky, damp-fleshed woman.

Born in Lancashire, England, **PENNY JORDAN** now lives with her husband in a beautiful four-teenth-century house in rural Cheshire. Penny has been writing for over fifteen years and has more than one hundred novels to her name, including the highly successful *To Love, Honor and Betray, Power Games* and *The Perfect Sinner.* With over sixty million books sold, and translations into sev-enteen languages, her record is truly phenomenal.

Penny Jordan

ONE INTIMATE NIGHT

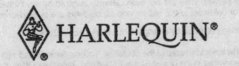

TORONTO • NEW YORK • LONDON
AMSTERDAM • PARIS • SYDNEY • HAMBURG
STOCKHOLM • ATHENS • TOKYO • MILAN • MADRID
PRAGUE • WARSAW • BUDAPEST • AUCKLAND

I should like to dedicate this book to everyone at the Cheadle and Cheadle Hulme Dog Club and, of course, to Sheba and Kerry.

ISBN 0-373-12146-6

ONE INTIMATE NIGHT

First North American Publication 2000.

Copyright © 2000 by Penny Jordan.

CHAPTER ONE

'GEORGIA...good... I'm sorry we've had to drag you in on your day off but there's a bit of a flap on.'

Georgia Evans's smile turned to an anxious frown as she saw the concern shadowing the eyes of the senior partner of the veterinary practice where she had worked since becoming a fully qualified vet six months earlier.

'I wasn't doing anything special,' she responded, ignoring the accusing mental image she had of her half-painted flat walls—a task she had willingly abandoned when she had received the telephone call from the surgery's receptionist asking if she could come in.

'What's—?'

Pre-empting her question, Philip Ross told her quickly, 'It's the mare out at Barton Farm; she's foaling and there are complications. Gary is with her but I suspect we may have to operate. I'm on my way over to join him now. Jenny will take over my morning's ops and Helen will take Gary's surgery, which will leave you as our emergency on-call vet, and if you could take the morning's dog-training class as well...'

As he spoke Philip was on his way out of the room, and, aware of the seriousness of the situation, Georgia made no attempt to delay him.

Once he had gone she walked into the main office and reception area of the practice.

Although all the small pets due to have operations had already been delivered by their owners, the main clinic of the day hadn't started as yet and Georgia was free to make herself a cup of coffee and check to see if she had any post, whilst discussing what had happened with the other two more senior vets she worked alongside.

'I hope we don't get any emergencies,' she confided to Jenny. 'I'm not sure...'

'If I were you I'd worry more about the dog-training class than any emergencies,' Jenny advised her wryly. 'Ben will be there...'

'Ben? Mrs *Latham's* Ben?' Georgia questioned, groaning when Jenny nodded.

'Oh, no!'

Mrs Latham's Ben was an English setter. A beautiful dog without an ounce of aggression in him, but unfortunately with more than his share of scattiness. To make matters worse Ben was a rescue dog, with Mrs Latham his second owner. Ben had been rescued from ending up in a dog's home thanks to her decision to give him a place to stay with her, and Georgia could well remember the first time she had seen him.

She had been working at the surgery for less than a month when a harassed young woman had turned up with Ben, who was just over a year old then and physically fully grown. He was a handsome, lovable, charming and completely dizzy dog, and Ben's then owner had complained to Georgia, who had been the vet on duty when she had brought him in, that with an elderly father to care for, a husband whose work took him away for days at a time and two young children she simply could not cope with a boisterous, energetic large dog.

As she'd looked from the woman's anxious eyes to the dog's trusting ones Georgia's heart had sunk. Ben was a beautiful dog, healthy, young, and as a fully bred pedigree had no doubt cost his owner an awful lot of money, but here she was telling Georgia defensively that there was simply no way she could keep him.

It had been at that moment that Mrs Latham had walked in, and Georgia's heart had sunk even further.

Mrs Latham was the owner of a raffish ginger tom cat who had adopted her when his previous owners had moved house. Ginger had cynically pounced on Mrs Latham's tender heart and the equally tender choice cuts of fish and meat she supplied him with and had moved himself in to Number One Ormond Gardens. But Ginger was, at heart, an independent warrior, and his night-time clashes with other cats in the neighbourhood meant that he was a regular visitor at the surgery.

Having reassured Mrs Latham that Ginger was recovering very well from the small operation he had had to repair a tear in his ear, Georgia had left Mrs Latham in the waiting room with Ben's owner whilst she went to collect Ginger from the cattery.

On her return she had discovered that Ben's owner had left but that Ben was still there, with a rather bemused Mrs Latham, who'd announced breathlessly to her that she was now Ben's new owner.

In vain had Georgia gently tried to dissuade her, pointing out all the problems she was likely to encounter with such a big dog in her small, pretty town house. Mrs Latham, however, had proved unexpectedly resistant to her arguments. Ben was now hers.

And so Ben had gone to live with Mrs Latham and Ginger, and a more indulged, pampered pair of pets, everyone at the surgery agreed, it would have been hard to find.

Ben, despite all Mrs Latham's attempts to 'train' him, was still regularly disrupting the weekly training class the surgery organised for dog owners.

'The problem is that Mrs Latham simply can't bring herself to be firm with Ben and show him who's boss,' Jenny had complained wryly after Ben had totally disrupted her own training session.

'He's a lovely dog but he needs a firm hand. As a breed, setters are scatty for the first two years. They need exercise and space and an owner who knows how to handle them. Mrs Latham loves him but she's sixty-two, and before Ben's eruption into her life she lived for her weekly bridge sessions.'

Helen had giggled. 'Has she told you about when she took Ben with her and apparently he was lying under the table and then got up at the wrong moment and sent it and the cards flying? He's banned from going now...'

Georgia, whose heart was just as tender as Mrs Latham's, had sighed.

'It's a shame, because he's such a lovely dog.'

'Try telling yourself that *after* you've taken a class with him in it,' Helen had advised her.

'I already have,' Georgia had told her, 'and I know just what you mean, but there's no malice in him; he's just—'

'He's just not the dog for a woman with Mrs Latham's lifestyle,' Helen had interrupted her.

It was true. Mrs Latham lived virtually in the centre of their small market town which, although quiet by modern-day standards, and surrounded by the farmland whose needs it serviced, was still no place for a dog who needed long, long country walks and a physically energetic owner.

Predictably, perhaps, Ben's original owner had proved impossible to trace—a 'visitor' unknown at the surgery. They had no record of either her or Ben.

They had all tried to suggest to Mrs Latham that a

new owner ought to be found for Ben, but still she'd refused to be swayed.

'He's already been abandoned once,' she had told Helen firmly. 'So traumatic for him, poor boy. Why, when he first came to me he was so frightened of being left that he insisted on sitting on my sofa right up next to me. So sweet...'

Helen had rolled her eyes at the others as she'd related this piece of canine emotional manipulation.

'So *sweet*,' she had scoffed. 'That dog knows when he's on to a good thing. Talk about spoiled...'

Smiling to herself now, Georgia picked up her post. A small, pretty girl with dark red curls and huge violet-blue eyes wide-spaced in a creamy-skinned, delicately small-boned face, she had wanted to be a vet ever since she could remember.

Getting this job in such a busy, prestigious practice and within a two-hour drive of her parents' home had been ideal, and she had soon settled down in the small flat she'd bought and begun to make new friends amongst her colleagues.

There was no man in her life: the years she had spent studying to qualify as a vet had meant that there had been neither the time nor the space for a permanent relationship. She had good friends, though—of both sexes—and enjoyed socialising. Ultimately she wanted to meet a special 'someone', fall in love, commit herself to their relationship and raise a family, but she was not in any hurry. Her warm personality and sensual good looks meant that she was never short of admirers. But right now her career was her main priority. Her elder brother often teased her that it was just as well that he was married with a young family because, otherwise, their parents would have had to wait a long time for their grandchildren.

Much as she loved her work, and the animals who featured in it, Georgia had no pet of her own, mainly because of the long hours she worked.

Quickly she checked her watch. Ten minutes to go before the owners and their dogs arrived for the week's training class.

This was an extra service the practice provided along with access, should their owners wish it, to a pet psychologist—every vet who took the class had to go on a special course themselves to make sure their own training skills were up to the mark. They ran two courses, one for adult dogs and one for younger puppies, and it was Georgia who normally took the puppy classes, which was a duty she loved.

The practice was very fortunate in that, having been established for many years, and initially having been set up by the present senior partner's grandfather, it owned the large garden to the rear of the Edwardian house which had been converted into its offices, operating theatre and surgeries. In addition to the cattery and kennels, the practice also had a large indoor training area, which was where the morning's class was to be held. Picking up her box of rewards, and making sure she had everything else she would need, Georgia opened the door and walked into the passageway which led to the training room.

Piers Hathersage grimaced as he surveyed the back seat of his once immaculate car, now covered in dog hairs and the papier mâché mess which had originally been a magazine he had inadvertently left there.

'Bad dog,' he told the culprit sternly.

Ben responded by barking sharply and rearing up on his hind legs. He was a powerful dog, and Piers wondered for the umpteenth time what on earth his godmother had been thinking of when she had decided to give him a home.

It was true that he was a very handsome dog—his coat shone and his eyes sparkled with humour, intelligence and mischief, whilst he bounded impatiently on his lead, trying to pull away in the opposite direction from which Piers intended to lead him.

Piers had arrived at his godmother's last night intending only to pay her a fleeting visit on his way back from his parents', but on finding that she had sprained her ankle whilst falling over her wretched dog, and that her main concern about her incapacity was the fact that she would be unable to take him to his weekly training class, he had felt obliged to offer to perform this chore for her.

'Oh, Piers, *would* you?' she had breathed with such evident relief. 'Do you hear that, Ben?' she had cooed at the miscreant.

'Uncle Piers is going to take you to your training class.'

Uncle Piers! Piers had gritted his teeth and manfully resisted the temptation to say what he was thinking.

Five months earlier, when his godmother had first got Ben, his parents had told him how concerned they were about the wisdom of her acquiring such a large, unruly dog.

'Why on earth *has* she got him?' Piers had asked them frowningly.

'Well, she was a bit vague on the subject,' his father had told him. 'However, it seems that he came to her via the veterinary practice where she takes that dreadful cat she's adopted.'

Piers's parents were both slightly younger than Emily Latham, who had befriended them as a young couple when they had first married.

Ten years ago, just after Piers had returned from a stint of working abroad, her husband had died and, remembering all the small kindnesses she had done for him as a boy and her generosity as a godmother, both with her time and her love as well, Piers had made sure that he continued to visit her just as often as he could.

She and her late husband had had no children, and Piers suspected it was because of this that she was inclined to have such a rose-coloured and sentimental view of children and animals.

Listening to his parents, Piers had well been able to imagine how easily she had been prevailed upon to take in someone else's abandoned dog, and he had further gathered from a chance remark of his godmother's that some young woman at the practice had been responsible for 'introducing' her to Ben. To encourage an elderly widow to take on a dog that was plainly quite unsuitable for her was, in his opinion, a highly irresponsible thing for *anyone* to do, much less someone who was supposed to be professionally involved with animals. But despite all his carefully logical arguments his godmother had remained obdurate: Ben was one of life's victims, a poor, misunderstood canine who, far from needing the strong hand of a firm disciplinarian, rather needed to have his psychoses treated with tenderness, love and indulgence.

Surveying the carnage Ben had wrought in his godmother's once immaculate garden, Piers had been unconvinced. However, his visit to Emily Latham had a dual purpose. Thanks to the increasing demand for the complex software programs produced by the business Piers ran, he was having to look for larger premises, and that had prompted him to consider moving away from the city, where he currently lived and worked, back to the town where he had grown up and where he knew that property was much less expensive.

He was, he reflected now, at the dangerous age of thirty-seven, not so very far off the landmark birthday of forty, and ready to eschew the fast-paced city life he had lived for the last decade for something a little gentler. He was also ready to trade the single life he had enjoyed, for something more companionable and cosy. A wife? Children? He wasn't *against* marriage as such, but perhaps he was too choosy because, as yet, he had not met 'the right woman', nor even come close to doing so.

Now, thanks to Ben and his godmother's painful ankle, he had had to put back the appointments he had made to view several properties in the area in order instead to take Ben to his training class.

'How many has he been to?' he had asked his godmother as she had tussled with Ben and the dog's reluctance to wear his collar, tenderly loosening it a notch.

'Oh, I'm not sure. I think this is his third. Of course, we did miss some of the classes in the first set I took him to. He got dreadfully upset because there was a dog there he didn't like, and the teacher suggested that it might be as well if he didn't attend for a few weeks. He was so disappointed, poor dog, and I really felt for him when all the other dogs graduated with good marks. He looked so downcast.'

'Oh, indeed,' Piers had agreed dryly, surveying the troublemaker with dispassionate eyes.

'He's a very sensitive animal,' his godmother had persisted gently. 'And *so* clever. He always knows when the telephone's going to ring and he comes to find me to tell me.'

Piers, who had heard the sorry tale of how the dog had chewed through the handset cord, had forborne to comment on this remarkable display of canine intelligence. His godmother always had been a soft touch.

Now, as he crisply commanded Ben to sit, he turned to investigate the mess of chewed paper on the rear seat and floor of the car, cursing under his breath as he realised the dog had munched on a magazine he had been keeping because of an article that contained some information he had wanted to reread.

Judging from the diverse array of cars in the practice's car park, its dog owners must span the full spectrum of human personalities, Piers acknowledged as his glance moved from a gleaming brand-new top-of-the-range Mercedes to a battered Land Rover and on to a pretty red and cream Citroën.

His own Jaguar was, he had to admit, a small piece of pure self-indulgence, a sleek dark maroon sports model which he had bought in a moment of uncharacteristic impulsiveness.

'What happened to the eco-friendly estate car you said you were intending to buy?' Jason Sawyer, his partner, had asked him wryly when he had seen it. Jason, with a wife and four children, often bemoaned the fact that the only really suitable car for his lifestyle was the large people-carrier which his wife drove, leaving him to use the family's second car.

'I'm not quite sure,' Piers had admitted.

'Enjoy it whilst you can,' Jason had told him. 'Belinda is making noises about us buying a camper

van. She says it will be ideal for touring holidays with
the kids!'

As Piers approached the entrance to the practice he
saw a large notice pinned to the door with an arrow on
it, stating 'Training Classes—this way.'

Following the direction of the arrow round the side
of the building, he could see a long, low range of out-
houses in front of him which had obviously been converted for a variety of uses. It was plain which one was
his destination from the small crowd of owners and dogs
milling around outside it, all of them surrounding a
small red-headed girl dressed in a white tee shirt that
lovingly moulded itself to her softly rounded breasts and
a pair of jeans which moulded themselves equally tenderly to a femininely curved bottom.

Very sexy, was Piers's first thought—his second was
that it was no wonder the majority of dog owners surrounding her were male.

It was obvious that she was the class's teacher, but
Piers deliberately held off from approaching her. It was
his habit to assess everything carefully and detachedly
before allowing himself to become involved with anyone. A little caution, in his view, was no bad thing, but
Ben, it seemed, had other ideas. A momentary lapse of
attention, a small slackening of Piers's firm hand on the
dog's lead, and Ben seized his chance.

Georgia had seen Ben and his unfamiliar human at-
tachment arrive out of the corner of her eye, but she
had been too busy welcoming her class with small treats
and warm words of welcome to pay too much attention—at least not openly. Inwardly, though, there was
nothing wrong with the speed of her reactions, nor the
lightning way that her senses registered the awesomely
male aspects of Ben's handler. Tall, broad-shouldered,

well muscled, if the way his tee shirt was being flattened against his torso by the breeze was anything to go by. Very thick short dark hair, a rather grim expression in those bitter-chocolate-brown eyes, it was true, and a certain very determined compression about the folded line of his mouth, but otherwise quite staggeringly good-looking, and more sexy in his jeans and tee shirt than any man except an actor as seen in a chocolate-bar advert had any right to be.

Ben, meanwhile, for reasons which only a similarly attuned canine mind could appreciate, had spotted the human who, so far as he was concerned, was responsible for his present blissful lifestyle in doggie heaven with Mrs Latham. He'd made a connection in his brain between Georgia's brief appearance in the waiting room at the vet's and his re-homing with Mrs Latham and, being the affectionate animal that he was, he quite naturally wanted to show his appreciation.

Having convinced his besotted owner that a collar worn anything less than loose enough for him to slip his head through and free himself from at will was an instrument of torture highly likely to cause him death by strangulation, as soon as he spotted Georgia he slipped his head from his collar with practised ease and tore across the yard towards her, scattering pets and owners as he did so, launching himself at Georgia and almost knocking her to the ground with the force of his enthusiastic greeting.

'Ben...down,' Georgia instructed firmly.

Tongue lolling, Ben obligingly wagged his tail.

'Ben,' Georgia repeated, 'down.'

Ben nuzzled her neck lovingly.

'Dr Dolittle, I presume,' Piers drawled sarcastically as he reached his escapee charge and unceremoniously yanked him off Georgia by the scruff of his neck, instructing him in an ominously quiet voice, 'Sit.'

Ben knew when a little diplomacy was called for. Obligingly he sat very heavily on Piers's feet, leaning lovingly against him and looking up into his eyes.

Ignoring this touching appeal, Piers sternly refastened Ben's collar—several notches tighter.

Georgia knew that it was up to her to take charge, but for some reason her thought processes seemed to have turned to gooey marshmallow. All she could focus on was how wonderfully broad Piers's chest was, how flat his belly, how corded with male muscles his arms were, as Ben twisted and turned in his hold, giving sharp, short barks of feigned distress.

'I don't know who was responsible for foisting this delinquent hound on my godmother,' Piers was saying through gritted teeth, 'but if I ever find out...'

So he was Mrs Latham's *godson*. Sternly reminding herself that she was a trained professional, and that right now her attention ought to be focused on her canine pupils and not on the six-foot hunk of hormone-level-raising male gorgeousness standing in front of her, Georgia dipped her hand into the box of rewards she had put down at her feet, proffering one to Ben.

'Good boy, Ben. Sit...' she cajoled him.

'Don't—' Piers began sharply, and then stopped as Ben suddenly turned into the most demure dog imaginable, giving Georgia a liquid-eyed look of love before taking the titbit she was offering him.

'Come on, everyone,' Georgia instructed her small group. 'Let's go inside and get started.'

Once inside the large, empty room it quickly became obvious to Piers that, whilst the majority of the other dogs there were responding to Georgia's careful instructions to their owners, when it came to doggy obedience Ben was in a class of his own.

When he had disrupted the class for the fifth time, by grinning wickedly at the slightly nervous collie bitch to one side of him and standing, Piers was quite sure deliberately, on the tail of the dog on the other side, Piers decided he had had enough.

There was no doubt about it: Ben was a master manipulator and most definitely not the dog for a woman as hopelessly incapable of disciplining him as his godmother.

Several yards away Georgia tried to keep her mind on what she was doing. Ben's waywardness was communicating itself to the rest of the class, and Georgia could see the sardonic look in Piers's eyes as the dogs grew restless, their concentration broken by Ben's sabotage.

Ben's trouble wasn't that he wasn't intelligent enough, Georgia reflected; it was more that he was *too* intelligent. Too intelligent and far too energetic for his current sedate lifestyle. Setters were gun dogs; they needed exercise and lots of it, and equally large amounts of firm handling.

The class came to an end and, as was her custom, Georgia made a point of going up to each dog to pet it before it and its owner left.

Ben she left till the last. *Not*, she assured herself, for any reason other than that she was curious to know why Mrs Latham had not brought him to the class.

'My godmother has hurt her ankle,' Piers informed Georgia curtly after she had introduced herself and asked him where Mrs Latham was.

Close up, Piers was even more excitingly masculine

than she had imagined. Stern, cold-eyed men were not normally her style, Georgia admitted; she preferred good humour to good looks any day of the week. But something was quite definitely causing that little quiver of female appreciation she could feel disturbing her normal level-headed calmness.

However, it was plain that Piers was nowhere near as impressed by her as she was by him, Georgia conceded ruefully as she heard him telling her curtly, 'If today's evidence of the success of your dog-training classes is anything to go by, I'm not surprised that Ben is proving so obdurate. Have you any professional qualifications for this?'

Immediately Georgia's hackles rose.

'I'm a fully trained vet,' she informed him shortly, 'and, yes, I have been trained to—'

'*You* may be trained, but Ben most certainly isn't,' Piers cut across her coldly. 'He's too much of a handful for my godmother, and...'

As she listened to him Georgia's heart began to sink. What he was saying was quite true, of course, but in his short life Ben had already had two homes and, despite his wilful determination to resist instruction, there was no doubt that in his own way he was devoted to Mrs Latham. Heavens knew what would happen to Ben if her godson were to persuade her to part with him.

Crossing her fingers mentally, Georgia told Piers semi-truthfully, 'Setters can initially be a bit wild, but once they get over that they calm down tremendously.'

'I'm sure they do,' Piers agreed, giving Georgia a narrow-eyed look, 'provided they are living in the right environment, and the right environment for Ben is not, in *my* opinion, the home of a sedentary woman who'll not see sixty again.'

'Ben has already been re-homed once,' Georgia told Piers protectively. 'It's a traumatic experience for a dog to be parted from an owner it's become attached to.'

'Indeed. However, I'm sure you'll agree that it would be an equally traumatic experience for my godmother if, as fortunately did *not* happen on this occasion, Ben were to pull away from her again and, instead of merely causing her to stumble and hurt her foot, dash out into the road with possible fatal consequences for himself.'

Georgia bit her lip. He *did* have a point, but she still felt she had to defend Ben.

'Once Ben can walk properly on the lead that kind of thing won't happen,' she informed Piers.

'Once! Don't you mean *if*, or more probably *never*?' Piers asked.

He looked down at the dog sternly. Ben smiled back at him, and then tensed as, out of the corner of his eye, he saw a cat strolling round the corner of the building. Springing to his feet, he tugged hard on his lead, forgetting that Piers had tightened his collar.

Piers gave an exclamation of irritation as Ben's leap for freedom caught him off guard and slightly off balance, and, instinctively knowing the dog's strength, Georgia reached out to grab hold of Piers's arm to help steady him.

Afterwards, Piers told himself that it was the feel of Georgia's soft breast pressing against him, the scent of her clean perfume in his nostrils and the softness of her hair brushing against his bare arm that had caused him momentarily to slacken his grip on Ben's lead. After all, Georgia *was* a stunningly attractive woman, and the sight of those soft, oh so well rounded breasts jiggling around inside her tee shirt whilst she had been running up and down the room with the dogs had left a lasting impression on his brain—and his body!

As Ben tore after the cat both Georgia and Piers shouted commands to him to stop, but it was Philip who was actually responsible for him coming to an abrupt halt as Ben turned the corner and ran full tilt into him.

Rushing across to take hold of Ben's lead, Georgia apologised to her boss.

'How is the mare?' she asked him anxiously.

'Fine. Both she and the foal are doing very well, although it was touch-and-go for a while.' Philip frowned as he turned from Georgia to Piers and asked, 'Isn't it Piers Hathersage?' He explained, when Piers acknowledged his recognition of him, 'I thought I remembered you from school. What are you doing these days?'

Discreetly Georgia left them to renew old acquaintanceships, at the same time making a mental note to ask Philip to have a word with Piers and hopefully persuade him to see Ben in a much better light than he currently did.

'He's not a bad dog,' she told Helen later, when she was relating to her what had happened.

'Not *bad*, no,' Helen replied, 'but you've got to admit that he is too much for Mrs Latham.'

'Mmm,' Georgia agreed. 'It's such a shame, though, because she's devoted to him and Ben thinks the world of her.'

'Oh, he's told you that, has he?' Helen teased her, adding, 'I think you're quite smitten with him yourself. Or is it someone else who has aroused your interest?'

Refusing to rise to Helen's bait, Georgia shook her head and exclaimed, 'Is that the time? I must go otherwise I shall be late for this afternoon's clinic.'

CHAPTER TWO

BY THE time he had driven Ben back to his godmother's, Piers had made up his mind. The dog had to go. However, when he let himself into the house he found Emily Latham in a state of some agitation. Her sister, it transpired, had telephoned her in Piers's absence asking her if she would like to take the place of her friend who had had to drop out of a three-week cruise of the Mediterranean at the last minute.

'Everything's paid for,' she told Piers. 'All I would have to do is pack and take the train to Mary's...'

'So what's stopping you?' Piers asked her with a smile.

Poignantly she looked at Ben.

'I just *can't* leave him,' she told Piers solemnly.

'You could put him in kennels,' Piers suggested.

Immediately his godmother shook her head.

'Oh, no, he'd hate that,' she told him, adding simply, 'Who would give him his chocolate at night and make sure he has everything he wants? No, he wouldn't be comfortable in kennels. He sleeps upstairs in my room at night and...'

Piers closed his eyes. It was getting worse and worse. No wonder the dog thought *he* was the boss.

'It's no good. I'll have to ring Mary and tell her I can't go,' Emily said dispiritedly.

Piers frowned and came to a quick decision. He had planned to spend only a few days with his godmother, looking at local properties, but, in reality, there was nothing to stop him from staying longer, nor from working from her house whilst he did so, and besides... He looked at the dog lying sprawled out on the rug in front of the fireplace, a whole array of semi-chewed toys spread around him.

With his godmother safely out of the way he could look around for another home for Ben.

'Yes, you can,' he told his godmother firmly. 'I'll stay here with Ben.'

'For three weeks? Oh, I couldn't ask you to do that,' Emily Latham demurred, but Piers could see the gleam of hope in her eyes.

'You aren't asking me,' he told her prosaically, 'I'm volunteering. And besides, it will give me more time to look around for somewhere to live and work.'

'Well, if you're sure...'

'I'm sure,' Piers confirmed. 'You go and ring Mary.'

As his godmother headed for the door she paused and stopped, saying, 'Oh, I nearly forgot. How did the training class go?'

Piers grimaced. 'It didn't. In fact the whole thing was shambolic. The young woman who took it was very easy on the eye and equally easy on the dogs. I always thought red hair was supposed to signify temper in a woman, but she—'

'Red hair... Oh, it must have been Georgia who took the class. She's lovely, isn't she? She's only been with the practice a few months. In fact it's really thanks to her that I got Ben...'

Piers tensed. 'Thanks to *her*? You mean *she* was responsible for that...that...?'

He stopped as the telephone started to ring and his godmother went to answer it. He might have *known*, he fumed. No wonder the wretched woman had been so keen to protect Ben, if she was the one who was responsible for his godmother having the dog in the first place. Of all the irresponsible...

Wrathfully he remembered the chaos of what had purported to be this morning's dog-training class. Philip must have used his eyes rather than his brain the day he had decided to employ her. She certainly was very eye-catching, with that mass of thick, dark red hair and that delicate face, those lusciously dark-lashed eyes and that body that was so curvy that it was just made for a man's hands to caress...

Abruptly Piers frowned; this was no way for him to be thinking. His godmother had more than likely committed the same folly of being instantly attracted to her crafty canine, for no one could deny that Ben *was* an extremely good-looking dog.

He, Piers, attracted to Georgia? Impossible... He liked cool, intellectual brunettes, tall and slim, fully up-to-speed independent women who would have shuddered in distaste at the mere thought of an animal's hair anywhere near their immaculately presented persons.

A short, curvy redhead with tousled curls who thought nothing of cuddling one of her furry friends was quite definitely not his cup of tea... No way...no way at all...

'That was Mary on the phone,' his godmother announced happily as she came back into the room. 'I've told her that I'm going to be able to join her after all.' Her face clouded slightly. 'Are you sure you *really* want to do this, Piers? I know that Ben can be rather a naughty boy at times, but his heart's in the right place...' She beamed adoringly at the dog, who had followed her into the room and was looking approvingly up at her.

'His heart may be, but unfortunately the rest of him does not appear to want to follow suit,' Piers murmured dryly, giving the dog a quelling look. Ben scratched vigorously behind his ear, causing Emily Latham to give Piers a horrified look of concern.

'Oh, Piers, you don't think he's caught something, do you?' she exclaimed worriedly.

'If he has I'm sure his friend at the vet's will be more than happy to relieve him of it,' Piers assured her grimly.

'Oh, dear, I'd better give them a ring, and then I must pack and you'll need food...and...'

'*I'll* ring them—in the morning. You go and pack by all means, but as for food I can shop for that myself tomorrow. This evening we'll eat out...my treat.'

'Oh, no...we *can't* do that,' his godmother protested. 'Not on my last evening at home. It wouldn't be fair to Ben.'

'No, of course not,' Piers agreed sardonically. 'I wasn't thinking. Do forgive me, Ben!'

'We could have a take-away,' Emily suggested. 'There's a very good pizza place in town that delivers. Ben loves them, don't you, Benny? He likes the anchovy ones best...'

Defeatedly Piers closed his eyes whilst Ben's tail thumped enthusiastically on the floor.

'Thanks for taking this afternoon's cases,' Philip told Georgia as she emerged from their second surgery. 'Oh, and by the way, if I could just have a word with you before you leave...?'

Despite Philip's smile and his thanks Georgia was conscious of a small frisson of unease. However, the afternoon's patients had all turned out to be fairly straightforward, and any who had needed minor treatment had all responded well.

'Ah Georgia.' Philip smiled as she popped her head round the door to his office a few minutes later. 'Yes…come on in…'

'Well, the good news is that you can take your missed day off tomorrow, if that suits you.'

'Yes, thank you, that will be fine,' Georgia accepted. 'The good news', he had said; that meant that there was some bad.

'Sit down,' Philip invited her, indicating the chair in front of his desk. 'I appreciate that you were somewhat thrown in at the deep end, so to speak, today, and I'm sure that, like all of us here, there are some aspects of the work you prefer to others. For instance I've always enjoyed operating and large-animal work, whilst Helen, as you know, prefers dealing with the smaller domestic pets…'

Georgia frowned, wondering where exactly Philip's conversation was leading. In another few seconds she knew.

'I understand that this morning's dog-training class wasn't entirely successful.'

Georgia's heart started to thump a little uncomfortably. Had someone complained?

'There were one or two problems,' she admitted huskily. 'Ben…'

'It does require a certain type of very strong personality to control a group of over-excited dogs,' Philip continued before she could explain. 'I know. I've been having a look at your file and I see that you had an excellent report from the intensive dog-training course we sent you on, but sometimes translating what has been learned in that kind of protected, cocooning environment into real life can be more difficult than we envisage.'

'Someone's complained.' Georgia couldn't help preempting him flatly. 'I know that things did get a bit out of hand this morning, but...'

'A bit!' Philip's eyebrows rose. 'According to Piers, the dogs were totally out of control.'

'Piers...' Georgia's heart thumped even harder. Oh, she might have known that he would be the one.

'The reason they were out of control,' she defended herself hotly, 'was because *he* had brought Ben.'

'Ben.' Philip sighed. 'Yes, I'm afraid Ben is proving to be rather a problem, and not just at the dog-training classes, according to Piers. I understand that he's recently been the cause of Mrs Latham hurting her ankle—fortunately not seriously—this time. But so far as Piers is concerned I suspect that Ben is very much on parole.'

Was that Philip's way of saying that so was she? Georgia wondered a little later as she drove home. Philip was a kind employer, and Georgia had thought she had found if not the idyllic then certainly an ideal job for herself, but Philip's gentle little homily this afternoon was making her wonder if the partners were as happy with her as she was with them.

Philip's last words to her had been a hint that maybe she might think it worthwhile doing a further intensive course in dog training. Only by reminding herself that the blame for her carpeting lay not with Philip, nor even with Ben, but with his irascible and unpleasant handler, had she been able to bite back the impulsive retort that had sprung to her lips that the one who needed the intensive course was not so much her but Ben.

He was a friendly and highly intelligent dog, but Mrs Latham spoiled him dreadfully.

With another three months to go before her nine-month probation period was fully up, Georgia now felt uncomfortably aware that her job might not be as secure as she had imagined. There were other veterinary practices, of course, but she *liked* this one, and besides, how was it going to look on her CV if the practice didn't give her a full-time contract? Not good—not good at all.

This was all down to Piers Hathersage, she reflected angrily.

The following day Georgia drove to Mrs Latham's home in the centre of the town.

It was late afternoon, and the early summer sunshine was throwing soft dappled shadows over the warm sandstone in which the local houses were built.

Wrexford was a charming place, a sturdily built and solidly settled market town which took a pride in itself and its history. The River Wrex, from which the town got its name, ran virtually through the town centre; originally the place had been the only spot where local people could ford the breadth of the river, and although modern-day traffic crossed it by bridge the local council had made an attractive park area along the river banks through the town centre for people to enjoy.

Mrs Latham's Queen Anne town house was one of a pretty terrace built originally by a local landowner and let out to the town's prosperous burghers.

The street leading to the houses was not open to general traffic; its modern tarmac covering had been stripped back to reveal the original cobblestones and traditional street lighting had been installed, complete with hanging baskets of pastel-coloured trailing plants. In front of the houses themselves the cobbled area opened out into a wider rectangle of ground reaching to the river, with a mature beech tree in its centre.

Residents and their visitors were allowed to park on the cobbles, although all the houses had long gardens and garages to their rear, and it was on these cobbles that Georgia parked her own small estate car, facing the river. Water had always fascinated her, and the River Wrex was a particularly attractive one, especially here in the town, where the very stringent conservation rules of the area meant that the water was blissfully clear and home to a wide variety of wildlife. During Georgia's first month at the practice someone had brought in an otter with a damaged paw which had been found on the river path. Thankfully a small operation had repaired the damage and the otter had been successfully returned to its home.

Upstream from the town, on the site of what had originally been the area's corn mill, the original buildings had been turned into a tourist attraction—the millpond cleaned out and its weir restored to its original glory. It was a popular site for picnickers and walkers and Georgia, who loved the countryside, couldn't help thinking how fortunate she was to live and work in such a beautiful environment.

She felt completely at home here, and had even begun to daydream of the admittedly at the moment remote possibility that she might one day be able to afford to buy into the partnership as a junior partner.

Under Philip's traditional management the practice had a slightly old-fashioned air to it, so Georgia had been thrilled when the response to her pleas to be allowed to introduce a pet-visiting scheme to a nearby old people's home had met with overwhelming success.

The pets, carefully chosen and nominated by their vets and accompanied by their enthusiastic owners, visited the home on a regular basis to see their human 'friends'.

One elderly man, who had always had a dog throughout his adult life before entering the home, had cried emotional tears to see the chocolate-brown Labrador who had visited him.

'He's just like my Brownie was,' he had told the dog's owner in a choked voice as he'd stroked the obliging dog.

Georgia had several other similar schemes she wanted to introduce as and when the opportunity arose. But with a black mark hovering over her, thanks to Piers, how *could* she do so?

It was pointless, of course, blaming Ben or Mrs Latham. Even so, she was hoping that the opportunity might arise to suggest tactfully to the older woman that both she and Ben would benefit from Ben undergoing a complete retraining course at the hands of someone with the expertise to teach the dog properly on a one-to-one basis.

Opening her car door, Georgia got out and walked determinedly towards Mrs Latham's house.

Piers was in the kitchen when Georgia rang the bell—and feeling rather out of temper. He had driven his godmother to the nearest mainline station earlier in the day and then gone on from there to do some essential food shopping. The diet of an old lady who, whilst not totally vegetarian nevertheless seemed to prefer a very light menu, was not one that he, as a six-foot, twelve-and-a-half-stone mature adult man felt happy with. Not that he didn't believe in healthy eating—he did—but he liked substantially more on his plate than his godmother enjoyed.

He had returned to her house via the estate agent's, where he had had an in-depth talk with the representative he had seen, outlining his requirements, and had come away with half a dozen promising property details to look over, feeling more than ready for the lunch of locally grown new potatoes accompanied by Scottish salmon, fresh vegetables and a hollandaise sauce he had promised himself.

His first intimation that this was to be a delayed pleasure had occurred when he'd opened the front door and seen the soft drift of feathers floating innocently down the stairs and into the hallway.

Feathers…!

He'd studied them frowningly as the draught of air from the open kitchen door drew them outside.

Feathers?

An unpleasant suspicion had gathered as ominously as the frown corrugating his forehead.

Putting down his shopping, he'd called out sternly, 'Ben?'

Silence…

Nothing…!

Closing the back door, Piers had hurried upstairs. The door to his godmother's bedroom was open, and as he'd looked into the room his heart had sunk. There was Ben, lying fast asleep on his godmother's bed, surrounded by feathers; a torn pillow on the floor had pointed to their origins and Piers had taken a deep breath before saying firmly, 'Ben!'

In his sleep the dog had breathed deeply, and then wrinkled his nose as a feather landed softly on it.

Grimly Piers had surveyed him. No way could the dog be asleep, and, as though to prove him correct, Ben had suddenly lifted one eyelid just the merest fraction and then closed it again.

Wrathfully Piers had taken action, marching over to the bed and getting hold of Ben's collar and yanking him firmly onto the floor.

Four hours later, having made do with a sandwich for his lunch, he had finally cleared away the last of the feathers, walked Ben, given him his meal and responded to his godmother's anxious phone call that, yes, he and Ben were getting on fine, albeit through fiercely gritted teeth.

Now, just as he was about to sit down and study the estate agent's properties, someone was at the door. No doubt some crony of his godmother's, who would want to have the full story of where she was and who he was.

Irritably Piers walked towards the hall door.

Immediately Ben got up to follow him. He was a sociable dog, and in his experience visitors to the house meant an hour or so of entertainment and the added attraction of some of Mrs Latham's home-made cake— plus, if he was really in her good books, his own special mug of tea. Ben liked tea.

Barking excitedly, his tail wagging furiously, he rushed past Piers, determined to get to the front door ahead of him. Well, after all, he was the main male of the household. That chancy cat didn't count. It had a home of its own several streets away, as Ben well knew, and only came here for extra meals.

As Ben made to barge past him Piers reacted immediately, grabbing hold of his collar and stopping him and then using it to half push and half drag the dog back into the kitchen, hauling him towards his bed and sternly telling him, 'Quiet... Stay.'

Unused to such cavalier treatment, Ben did exactly that for just as long as it took Piers to get on the other side of the door and close it, and the sound that greeted Georgia as Piers opened the door to her was one of heart-rending distress as Ben, recovering from Piers's assault to his household supremacy, started to howl with a piteous and searing intensity.

'What's happened? What's wrong with Ben? What have you done to him?' Georgia demanded immediately, her glance going anxiously to the closed kitchen door, behind which the dog's agonised wails were increasing in volume.

'I haven't done anything to him,' Piers denied sharply. 'What—?'

'Yes, you have. You've hurt him,' Georgia insisted, ignoring Piers to hurry to the kitchen door and push it open.

As soon as he saw her Ben's eyes lit up. This was more like it—a human who understood! Whining pitifully, he lay in his basket, his eyes half closed whilst he breathed arduously.

Whilst Piers looked on grimly from the doorway, Georgia rushed over to Ben, getting down on her knees in front of him, quickly checking his pulse and then the rest of him.

To her relief nothing seemed to be wrong, and then, disconcertingly, just as she was about to demand an explanation for his piteous cries from Piers, Ben opened one eye and started to nuzzle hopefully at the pocket where she kept her dog treats.

From behind her Georgia heard Piers saying sardonically, 'It seems that diagnosis is even less your forte than training... There's nothing wrong with him.'

'Where's Mrs Latham?' Georgia demanded, hot-faced with chagrin. Piers, it seemed, was quite right—there was nothing wrong with Ben, but there was no way she was going to admit as much.

'Not here, I'm afraid. Nor will she be here for the next few weeks; she's having a much needed holiday with her sister, and whilst she's away I'm going to be staying in *loco parentis*, so to speak.'

'She's left Ben with you? *You're* looking after him?' Georgia queried, unable to hide her feelings.

'There wasn't really much alternative. It seems that the kennels weren't...er...able to take him...'

Georgia's flush deepened a little as she saw the way Piers was looking at her.

'You're staying here, looking after Ben?' she repeated, swallowing tensely, as though she found the words uncomfortably unpalatable.

'I'm staying here looking after Ben,' Piers agreed grimly. 'And whilst I'm here I am going to look round for a more suitable home for him.'

'No!' Georgia protested. 'You *can't* do that. Mrs Latham would never part with him.'

'My godmother is besotted with the animal, I agree,' Piers replied acidly. 'But that does not make theirs in any way a suitable alliance. Far from it...'

'It isn't Ben's fault he's so...so...so disruptive,' Georgia defended. 'If he was properly trained—'

'*If* he was properly trained. But that's the crux of the matter, isn't it? He is most certainly not in *any* way trained at all, and in my view—'

'Setters *are* scatty when they're young...but...'

Georgia had no idea why she was defending the dog so fiercely. After all, she had said herself that Ben wasn't really a suitable dog for Mrs Latham, but something about the way Ben was looking at her, something about the obvious love and the doggy treats and toys which surrounded him touched her heart in a way she could hardly explain to herself, never mind to the tough, uncompromisingly unemotional man standing in front of her.

'Look, I appreciate that you have a vested interest in him staying here. After all, you were the one who foisted him on my godmother in the first place, weren't you?' Piers told her grimly.

Georgia stared at him.

'No. I...'

'Don't bother trying to deny it,' Piers warned her. 'My godmother told me herself that you were responsible for her getting Ben.'

Georgia's heart sank. Mrs Latham *had* on more than one occasion mentioned how large a part she believed Georgia's unavoidable absence from the waiting room had played in her becoming Ben's new owner. But for Piers to claim that she had either actively solicited such a situation or even encouraged it was way beyond the truth. Not that she was going to attempt to tell him so. Why should she? Let him think badly of her if he wished. *She* didn't care; why should she?

Just because he had the kind of sexy good looks that made her heart thud and her temperature rise, that did *not* mean that she was foolish enough to want to solicit his good opinion and ignore her own principles in doing so. Besides, he really wasn't her type. No, not at all. She liked men with kind, open, honest faces and ready smiles, men who liked animals and understood them.

The kind of man she liked would have immediately seen that Ben was as much a victim of the situation as his owner.

Georgia frowned as she looked down at Ben. She had no doubt that Piers would carry out his threat to find him a new home. And if he *couldn't*... A horrible mental picture of Ben being dragged into the surgery to face... Georgia swallowed hard. The practice had a rule about not destroying healthy dogs simply because their owners no longer wanted them. But there were *other* practices... Tears filmed her eyes. Quickly she ducked her head and blinked them away. There was no way anything like that was going to happen to Ben. Not whilst *she* was around to prevent it.

'All Ben needs is someone with the skill and the patience to treat him properly. He's a strong-willed dog but there's no malice or unkindness in him.'

'*Someone.*' Piers raised his eyebrows. 'And have you any suggestions where I might find this paragon?'

Both his voice and his expression implied that he already knew that such a task was way beyond *her* capabilities, and, remembering the chaos of yesterday's training class, Georgia could understand why.

'He's a very intelligent dog,' she persisted. 'He *could* be trained.'

'But not by you, apparently,' Piers told her derisively.

Georgia felt her face burn with discomfort. When she had finished her training course the instructor had told her that he had been impressed with her ability to handle the dogs. 'But you could be a little bit firmer,' he had added.

'If I had him on a one-to-one basis then, yes, I could train him,' Georgia insisted recklessly.

There was a long silence, and then, to her consternation, Piers said coolly, 'Very well, then, prove it. You've got three weeks to persuade me that you're right.'

Three weeks. Georgia swallowed nervously. What on earth had she done? What on earth had she committed herself to? There were places, she knew, where dogs underwent two-week intensive training courses, guaranteed to have them obeying all the basic commands and walking to heel, but the dogs were boarded at the training school and the trainers spent all day, every day, teaching them. There was no way she could achieve anything like the same effect with a couple of training sessions twice a week for three weeks.

'It isn't quite that easy,' Georgia protested. 'To train him properly I'd have to have him living with me, and I'm not allowed to have a pet in my flat.'

'Admit it. You *can't* train him,' Piers challenged her.

Georgia's eyes darkened to deep purple with the passion of her emotions. 'I could if I had him living with me,' she repeated. 'But, as I've just told you, that isn't possible.'

'Maybe not, but it *is* possible for *you* to come and live with *him.*'

'Live with him...?' Georgia stared at Piers.

'My godmother has another guest bedroom, and I'm sure, under the circumstances, she wouldn't have any objection to your moving in here for the duration.'

'Me...move in here...with *you*?' Georgia squeaked.

'No,' Piers corrected her gently. 'You move in here to train Ben.' And then, even more gently, he explained, 'If *I* was inviting you to move in *anywhere* with me, I promise you the necessity for a spare guest bedroom would not exist!'

Her face scarlet with mortification, Georgia scrambled to her feet.

'I can't move in here,' she said—but then her glance fell to Ben, who was lying peacefully at her feet. He really was the most handsome dog, and his nature was so devoid of any kind of meanness that he deserved a loving owner and a good home. And there was no doubt about the rapport which existed between him and Mrs Latham, even if he did take atrocious advantage of her.

The thought of him being passed on to yet another owner or ending up unwanted in a dogs' home was just too much for Georgia's tender heart to bear.

'I'll do it,' she heard herself saying recklessly. 'I'll move in and I'll prove to you just how well-trained a dog Ben can be...'

The derisive look Piers was giving her warned Georgia that he had scant faith in her claim, but that only made her feel all the more determined to prove herself and Ben to him.

Mentally she started to make plans. Coincidentally she had some holiday leave due. If she took it that would give her some extra time with Ben. The practice was within walking distance of Mrs Latham's house, so she would be able to dash home during her break when she was working to be with him, and then there were her off-duty hours. Three weeks. She could feel the anxiety starting to clutch at the pit of her stomach.

'Second thoughts?' she heard Piers asking her sardonically.

'No,' she denied firmly. 'But *you* will have—once Ben's trained.'

'I shan't hold my breath,' Piers advised her dryly.

CHAPTER THREE

'YOU'RE doing *what*?' Helen asked Georgia in startled amazement the next day, when Georgia told her what had happened.

'Not *doing*, have already done,' Georgia corrected her wryly. 'I moved into Mrs Latham's house yesterday afternoon.'

'So you're living with Piers? Mmm...lucky you,' Helen teased her, rolling her eyes expressively. 'If I didn't love David so much...'

'I am not *living* with *anyone*,' Georgia contradicted her swiftly. 'I'm simply staying there so that I can train Ben. He's such a lovely dog, really, Helen, but Piers is determined to put pressure on his godmother to make her get rid of him; I can tell. It will be a strictly business relationship.'

'I just hope you know what you're doing,' Helen told her warningly. 'You know how keen Philip is on maintaining the right image for the practice, and he does tend to be a little bit old-fashioned. He won't take it very well if you don't succeed—your failure reflecting on the reputation and good name of the practice et cetera, et cetera—even more so, I feel, since Piers has put it on a business footing.'

'Well, I'm under a cloud in Philip's books already, thanks to Piers,' Georgia admitted. 'But I can't just let him cold-bloodedly send Ben away. Which reminds me, I'm going to have to skip lunch today; I want to go back to the house and do some work with Ben. I took him for a good long walk before I came out this morning.'

'You did?' Helen raised her eyebrows. 'Well, that has to be an achievement all by itself. According to Mrs Latham he hates wearing a collar and pulls like mad on a lead.

'You did use a lead, didn't you?' she demanded when she saw the way Georgia was avoiding looking at her.

'It was very early in the morning. No one else was about on the river path and I managed to bribe him to come back with some treats,' Georgia told her defensively. 'He needed the exercise, Helen; that's part of the trouble. He isn't using enough energy.'

'Mmm...' was all Helen would allow herself to say.

Piers had been equally unimpressed by the fact that she had walked Ben off his lead. It had been unfortunate that he should have been in the kitchen when she had arrived back with the dog and had seen her coaxing him back into the house with treats.

'I think my godmother has already taught him that particular message,' Piers had told her grimly as Ben had refused to come more than a few feet at a time without extra treats. 'If this is your idea of training him, then—'

'He *needed* a walk,' had been all Georgia would permit herself to say as she'd prepared Ben's food.

When she had returned to the house the previous day, Piers had been waiting for her and had shown her upstairs to a delightful bedroom complete with its own bathroom.

'I'm up on the next floor,' he had informed her, lifting his head in the direction of the ceiling, 'so we shouldn't be under one another's feet too much. Tomorrow, once you've had time to settle in, I suggest we draw up a timetable which will allow us both to use the kitchen in privacy, although most evenings I shall probably be eating out.'

Georgia hadn't said anything for the simple reason that she'd desperately been trying to assimilate the import of the strong surge of disappointment his words had brought her. What was the matter with her? Surely she didn't want to share her meals with him? Surely she didn't want to share *anything* with him? How could she after the antagonism and, yes, *dislike*, he had shown towards her?

He had also outlined to her the reason why he was staying in his godmother's house, underlining the fact that when he was working he preferred to do so without any kind of interruption.

'I wouldn't dream of interrupting you,' Georgia began stiffly, but fell silent with fury when he continued as though she hadn't spoken.

'Naturally I have no desire to pry into your...private life, but suffice it to say that I also feel it is something that should be conducted in your *own* home.'

'If you're suggesting that I would...that I have—' she began, and then stopped, contenting herself with a curt, 'I don't happen to have the kind of "private life" I suspect you mean, but *if* there was someone... special...in my life...I can assure you that there is no way I would want to see him or be with him, with you...' She stopped again as her words threatened to choke her. 'Anywhere other than...somewhere I could be completely private with him,' she told Piers shakily.

How dared he suggest that she would indulge in...that she would want to...? The very thought...

Piers watched her with a small frown. There was no mistaking either her sincerity or her vehemence, just as there was equally no mistaking the fierce surge of male pleasure it gave him to know that not only was there no man in her life but also that her attitude betrayed the fact that her sexual experience was probably limited to little more than one relationship—a youthful affair with a fellow student, which she had begun as a virgin and left, though technically a 'woman', with very little real experience of true sensuality.

Georgia would have been shocked and chagrined to know what he was thinking, mainly because his thoughts were so accurate. Losing her virginity to her boyfriend at university had seemed to be the right thing to do. She had liked Mark, had trusted him, and had even persuaded herself that she loved him. And for a while perhaps she had, but her sexual intimacy with him had left her feeling that there must be something lacking in her that she should have found it so pedestrian an experience, almost totally lacking in the fireworks and intensity she had imagined. They had parted amicably after just over a year together—Georgia had no regrets about the fact that they had been lovers, only about her own failure to experience the sensations, to feel the ecstasy others seemed so capable of achieving.

Piers had given her her own key to the house and had passed on to her the detailed verbal instructions his godmother had given him as to Ben's routine and care.

'He has *what*?' Georgia had demanded in bemusement at one point.

'Bakewell tart on Mondays, cream sponge on Wednesdays and chocolate éclairs on Fridays. Apparently *they* are his favourite,' Piers had told her sardonically. 'Oh, and he likes to wash them down with a mug of tea…'

'Tea. Well, yes, some dogs *do* like it,' Georgia had agreed.

What she couldn't understand was how Ben managed to stay so healthy-looking and fit on such a patently unhealthy diet and with so little exercise, but when she'd said as much to Piers he'd told her grimly, 'Oh, but he *does* have plenty of exercise. Nearly every day, according to my godmother, he manages to escape from the garden, often not returning for close on an hour...'

Which was why she had recently had installed a new dog-proof fence made of strong netting. Georgia had recommended to Mrs Latham that she wire in an underground electric fence, operated via a special unit attached to Ben's collar, but Mrs Latham had considered it too dangerous for the darling animal!

Georgia had closed her eyes. She really hadn't wanted to hear any more!

Now she glanced at her watch. It was time for her break.

Ben greeted her with a welcome bark when she let herself into the house, launching himself at her and trying to lick her enthusiastically.

'Down, Ben,' she commanded. 'Down...'

Predictably Ben ignored her. Suppressing a sigh, Georgia went to open the back door. Obligingly Ben followed her.

'Sit, Ben,' she commanded once they were outside. Obediently Ben did so.

Amazed, as well as pleased, Georgia went to praise him and give him a treat, but as she reached him Ben nimbly sidestepped her and, with startling speed, raced towards the other end of the garden.

'Patience and perseverance,' Georgia repeated determinedly to herself under her breath half an hour later as Ben, having thoroughly enjoyed the game of racing up and down the garden whilst Georgia tried to get him to sit still, stood two feet away from her, tongue lolling, grinning widely.

Georgia closed her eyes and took a deep breath before commanding firmly, 'Sit, Ben. Sit.' She grasped his collar with one hand and placed her other firmly on his back.

Ben was a strong dog, though, and from the start it was equally plain to both of them that he was going to win the undignified tussle which ensued. Well, at least Piers wasn't here to witness Ben's triumph over her, she told herself as Ben finally grew tired of the game and, with a strong tug, almost pulled her off her feet, causing her to tumble and end up sprawling on the grass.

Her break was over, and so far she had made absolutely no progress whatsoever. Tonight after work she would try a different tack, she promised herself as she managed to coax Ben back into the kitchen before quickly tidying herself up. A long, long walk to burn off some of his energy followed by some walking-to-heel training, and whilst she had him on his lead they could practise some sitting on command as well.

'How did it go?' Helen asked her when she was back at work.

'Don't ask,' Georgia responded wearily.

'Mmm...well, I looked out a couple of animal psychology books for you,' Helen told her. 'Perhaps they might help.'

'If Ben continues to behave the way he did this lunchtime *I'm* going to be the one needing the psychologist,' Georgia told her feebly.

'Remember, per—'

'Perseverance and patience, I know,' Georgia agreed. 'Only Ben already has them both.'

Before leaving work that evening Georgia made a few necessary purchases: a short choke chain to replace Ben's collar and lead, and some more treats.

Since her training session with Ben had not left her enough time for lunch she was feeling extremely hungry. She had made some chilli the previous day and she was looking forward to eating it along with some of the delicious fresh bread she had bought from the local bakery. However, the first thing that hit her as she walked into the house was the delicious, mouth-watering smell of cooking food. Her stomach started to rumble. Piers was obviously back before her. For some reason she had expected to return before him, and besides, hadn't he said that he normally ate out?

As she pushed open the kitchen door the first thing she saw was Ben's empty bed, the second Piers himself, who was standing beside the open oven door stirring something inside it.

'What have you done with Ben?' she demanded anxiously, her glance swivelling back to the empty bed.

'I've put him outside until after I've had my supper,' Piers informed her grimly.

'What...? Why...? That's...' Georgia stopped as her stomach rumbled protestingly again, and so loudly that she knew Piers must have heard it.

'Didn't you eat lunch?' Piers asked her, his eyebrows raised.

'I...I didn't have time... I...I was training Ben...'

'Ah...' The look Piers was giving her spoke volumes, and Georgia could feel her face starting to burn.

'Yes, quite successfully actually,' she fibbed defiantly, tossing her head.

'Mmm...I saw you,' Piers told her, to her consternation.

'Y-you saw me?' Georgia stammered. 'But you couldn't have done; you were out...'

Calmly Piers shook his head. 'No,' he corrected her. 'I was upstairs working... Tell me...just where in the training manual does it encourage allowing the dog to get *you* to sit...or were you simply demonstrating to him what you required him to do?' he asked sarcastically.

Angrily Georgia gritted her teeth. There was nothing she could say—not right now. Let him taunt her—it would only make her all the more determined to prove him wrong.

'You mentioned something about drawing up a rota for using the kitchen,' she told him stiffly. 'Perhaps when you've finished your meal...'

She'd seen the look he gave her as she'd stressed the word 'you', but, instead of retaliating, to her astonishment he simply said, 'I think on this occasion it might facilitate matters if we ate together. There's enough for two.'

She was going to refuse. Georgia knew that she had even opened her mouth to do so. But, for some unexplainable reason, the words that actually came out turned out to be a husky acceptance of Piers's unexpected offer.

'It's chicken in white wine sauce with new potatoes and salad,' he informed her. 'But if you don't—'

'It sounds delicious,' Georgia assured him quickly.

Ten minutes later she was able to confirm that the chicken tasted as delicious as it had sounded.

She had a good healthy appetite, something very rare in her sex in Piers's experience, and he watched her enjoy her meal with a relish that was totally innocently sensual. Everything about her glowed with good health, from the shine of her curls to the peachy gleam of her skin. Naked, her body would be firm and warm-fleshed, her breasts high and full, her waist so narrow he could span it with his hands, her hips flaring into the feminine curves of her thighs. Would the silky curls protecting her sex be as richly coloured as those on her head? Piers realised with a sharp jolt just where his thoughts were taking him and got up from the table, asking Georgia tersely, 'Coffee?'

A little uncertainly Georgia nodded in acceptance, wondering what it was she had done that had caused him to frown so fiercely—and why she should care.

'The chicken was delicious. Thank you,' she told him formally as she too got up and carried her plate over to the sink, to rinse it before placing it in the dishwasher. Once she had finished this chore she added, as she heard Ben scratching furiously at the back door, 'I'd better let him in.'

Piers made no comment, merely pouring boiling water on to the coffee and then waiting until Georgia had opened the door to admit Ben before asking her, 'Milk?'

'Mmm...please...' Georgia began, her back to the dog as she turned to respond to Piers's question, her answer turning to a startled gasp as Ben rushed full tilt into her, knocking her completely off balance.

Immediately Piers swung round, reaching out to grab hold of her, and instinctively Georgia steadied herself by grasping his arms, her head bumping against the solid wall of his chest with the force of Ben's enthusiastic response to being allowed inside.

It was only the way Piers had braced himself to catch her as she fell that was responsible for the fact that she was virtually lying full-length against him, her body pressed so close to the hard strength of his that it would have been impossible to pass a piece of paper between them. That was *all,* Georgia warned herself sternly. Just as it was only to support her that his arms were now wrapped tightly round her, almost as though he was cradling her tenderly within them. There was no doubt even a practical reason for that fierce, accelerated thud she could feel as his heartbeat picked up.

But her body seemed waywardly determined to interpret all these things in a very different way altogether. Cerebrally it might be implausible to believe that Piers was holding her like a lover, but her body was reacting to him as though he was. Embarrassingly so, Georgia realised as she felt her nipples become rigid, and the hot wave of shame washing down her body from her pink-cheeked face crashed into the even more intense surge of sensual awareness that was sweeping upwards over her skin.

'Oh, thank you,' was all she could find to say as she lifted her head from its resting place against Piers's deliciously solid chest and forced herself to look up into his face. After all, she had to say something to him for saving her from a nasty fall.

Her glance wavered treacherously on its upward journey, for some dangerous reason deciding to linger over his mouth, which for once was curled into a smile and not tightening into his customary frown. And *what* a smile! Feathers of delicious but oh, so dangerous sensations drifted through Georgia's stomach—tiny, barely perceptible tendrils of delicate pleasure that were somehow still strong enough to trap and enmesh her, making her feel light-headed and dizzy as well as a whole host of other things she didn't dare allow herself to name.

'Georgia…'

Piers's voice seemed to reach her from a long way

away, a husky resonance that vibrated thrillingly
through her whole body.

'Yes—' Her lips parted in her acknowledgement,
starting to form the word but never finishing it because,
impossibly, Piers's mouth was brushing softly against
hers. It was the merest tantalising movement, the tiniest
suggestion that it could turn into something far more
intense and intimate, but her body seemed to be decod-
ing its message with an instinct, an *insistence*, and immediately it sent her heart rate into triple speed, her
breath catching in her lungs as her own lips seemed to
cling provocatively to Piers's.

Now she knew why it was that Victorian women had
swooned so often when their lovers had kissed them,
Georgia decided dizzily as she looked bemusedly up at
Piers through half-closed eyes.

'Mmm...'

Was that soft purr of appreciation really coming from
her own throat? Were those really her own arms that
had wound themselves so tightly around Piers? Was that
really *her* body that was reacting to him...to *him*...with
all the ardency, all the excitement, all the expectancy
she had so longed to feel with Mark but which, in reality, she had never come anywhere near experiencing?

And, most importantly of all, was she really going to
waste time on foolish mental conundrums when there
were far more rewarding and pleasurable things to do?
When the increasingly determined exploration of Piers's
mouth was teaching hers a whole new world of sensual
discovery? Slowly his lips caressed hers, and even more
slowly his tongue explored their shape and softness. One
of the hands which had saved her from her fall was now
supporting the back of her neck, stroking through her
soft curls, cupping the delicate line of her jaw. His

mouth, then momentarily lifted from hers as his thumb pressed gently against the fullness of her bottom lip, exposing its velvety, sensitive inner flesh.

Shakily Georgia closed her eyes completely as she felt her body's response to what he was doing. How could such a simple gesture, such a simple *touch*, be capable of making her feel like this, *want* like this?

Piers's mouth had replaced his thumb, his tongue probing the softness it had just exposed and then going beyond it with a devastating intimacy that shocked through her body like an electric current.

'Oh-h-h!'

With a small startled protest Georgia realised that Piers was releasing her.

'You shouldn't have done that,' she told him unsteadily as she realised what *she* had done.

'No,' Piers drawled, giving her a narrow-eyed look that encompassed not just her well-kissed, swollen mouth but her equally swollen breasts as they pressed against the soft fabric of her tee shirt. 'Perhaps I wouldn't have done if you hadn't…invited me… It takes two, you know, and…'

Her invite *him*! Georgia made an angry, protesting sound of denial deep in her throat.

'I did not—' she began, and then stopped as Ben started to bark impatiently. 'I have to walk Ben,' she told him stiffly.

'Well, I shall probably be out when you return,' Piers told her dismissively. 'I've got a couple of properties I want to see this evening. Which reminds me, I shall be away all day tomorrow.'

'Good, I'm glad to hear it,' Georgia muttered grimly in what she had thought was a voice too low for him to hear.

But, to her chagrin, he *had* heard her, and in retaliation he told her silkily, 'Really? That wasn't the message I was getting a few minutes ago... In fact—'

'*You* were the one who kissed *me*,' Georgia told him hotly, immediately on the defensive.

Piers was silent for so long that at first she thought she had got away with it and that he wasn't going to say anything, but when he did she realised how much she had underestimated him.

He told her softly, 'A woman doesn't have to instigate a kiss to let a man know she wants one, and the way you looked at me...'

Without waiting to hear any more Georgia hurried to the back door, calling quickly to Ben as she did so.

Shamingly she knew that he did have a point. She *had*, albeit unintentionally, looked at his mouth for just that little bit too long, but she had never for one minute had any preconceived notion of doing so to provoke him into kissing her. *Never* for one single minute. No, the thought had never even crossed her mind. Why should it? They were antagonists...on opposite sides—she for *Ben*, Piers against him.

Through the kitchen window Piers watched Georgia coaxing Ben into his choke lead and then rewarding the dog with an affectionate pat and some kind of treat when he complied.

She would never succeed in training him in three *months*, never mind three weeks, Piers decided. She was far too soft. Ben was a dog used to having his own way, used to ruling the roost and dominating the household and his owner. What Ben needed was another, more determined male presence in his life.

Almost absently Piers noted the way Georgia's jeans

hugged the slim length of her legs and the rounded curve of her bottom. She had felt every bit as good in his arms as he had imagined, but not quite as good as she would have done had they been naked together in bed. Her skin had smelt of fresh air and peaches, and as he'd kissed her he had had a fierce surge of male desire to taste more of her, to strip that neat, high-necked tee shirt from her body and expose the delicious fullness of her breasts to his gaze...his hands...his mouth...

There was a decidedly potent male ache in his lower body, a decidedly testosterone-driven urge to take what had happened between them further—a whole lot further—threatening his normal cool control. When he had gone upstairs earlier, as he'd crossed the landing heading for the stairs which led up a further flight to his own quarters, there had been a very tantalisingly feminine scent in the air, a provocative, delicate woman smell that had sent his hormones into overdrive.

And she wasn't even his type. That red hair, that curvy body, that obvious inexperience in those bewitching dark pansy eyes—they weren't for him. No way...no way at all; and even if they had been there was one insurmountable barrier between them in the shape of that idiotic dog. The very barrier which had propelled her into his life...and into his arms...in the first place.

Emptying the cup containing Georgia's now cold cup of coffee, he grimaced over the unappetising taste of his own, pouring that away as well.

After one had tasted nectar, coffee had no appeal at all.

CHAPTER FOUR

'So...?' Helen asked Georgia three days later. 'Are you making any progress with Ben?'

'Some,' Georgia told her cautiously. 'He definitely understands the commands—he's a very intelligent dog—but getting him to respond to them is still something of a hit-and-miss affair. He walked beautifully on his lead last night, and sat on command.'

'Sounds good,' Helen approved, 'and I've got some more good news for you as well.'

Listening to her, Georgia acknowledged ruefully that Ben had somewhat spoiled his good performance the previous day by slipping free of his collar and chasing after a squirrel which had promptly run up a tree and bombarded him with prickly unripened chestnuts.

'The local paper has got wind of your dog visits to the old people's home and they want to run an article about it. Philip's keen for you to let them interview you and take some photographs of the owners with their dogs, kind of thing. It would be good publicity for us as well as a good public relations exercise. I'll leave it to you to nominate and contact the owners, and the reporter from the *Community News* will be in touch with you direct.'

Things were beginning to look up a bit, Georgia decided a little later as she walked back to her temporary new home, even more so since she hadn't seen Piers since that embarrassing incident in the kitchen. He had telephoned her from the city to say that he wasn't going to be able to return for a further couple of days, and Georgia had sturdily assured herself that the feeling she had had of a sharp sense of disappointment was nothing of the sort, that the problem owed its existence to the fact that she had gone without lunch—again!

She had quickly made use of the opportunity he had given her by concentrating Ben's training sessions in and around the house—much easier to do without Piers's critical presence and even more critical eye on what she was doing. Ben *was* an intelligent dog—certainly intelligent enough to sneak himself upstairs the first night she had been in the house alone and to hide himself under his mistress's bed whilst Georgia searched the house and then the garden for him!

The only reason she had finally realised what he had done had been that the sound of something falling to the floor upstairs with a muffled soft thud had caused her to go and investigate its cause, only to find Ben contentedly spread out on Emily Latham's bed, the noise she had heard caused by him accidentally dislodging a bedside lamp as he had jumped up. Fortunately the lamp hadn't been damaged, but Ben hadn't been too pleased about being removed from his self-chosen comfortable bed and returned to his legitimate quarters in his basket in the kitchen.

When she finished work today she intended to take Ben for a good long walk along the river before returning to the house for an intensive training session with him.

They were having a busy week at the practice, with a rush of new patients, kittens and puppies in the main, needing their protective injections.

To Georgia's distress, though, one elderly dog they had been treating for cancer was found to have developed another tumour, and his owner had to be gently informed that for the animal's own sake it would be kinder to have him put to sleep.

The owner, a widower, who had only taken the dog in at the insistence of his late wife, had, as he confided to Georgia, become far more attached to the dog than he had ever expected.

'We didn't have any children,' he told Georgia sadly, 'and Rex here is really my last living contact with my late wife. We were teenage sweethearts and married for fifty-four years. It's been two years now since I lost her, but I still miss her...'

Georgia's tender heart ached for him, but she had seen the dog Rex's X-rays and knew that there was no way the dog could survive.

It was always hard telling an owner that they were going to lose a much loved pet, all the more so because they always tried to take it so bravely, insisting that their pet's needs must come before their own desire to prolong its life.

Sometimes, though, they did see the other side of pet ownership—people who abused or neglected their animals. People like Ben's original owner, who acquired a puppy or a kitten and then blithely announced that it wasn't what they wanted after all and it would have to go.

Ben had been lucky in finding a second home, a second owner like Mrs Latham, but had she been similarly fortunate in acquiring Ben? Georgia doubted that her godson would have said so.

Piers. There she was thinking about him again. In fact, she was spending far too much time thinking about him altogether, and not just thinking about him in terms of the threat he represented to Ben's future. Georgia had to admit that she wouldn't have liked to have been keeping a list of just how many times her thoughts had drifted to those disconcerting moments she had spent in Piers's arms.

She was thinking about it—and Piers—two hours later as she made her way back to Mrs Latham's. Piers was due to return this evening. Would he be there when she got back from work or would he return later?

One thing she did know was that when he did come back he would be watching both her and Ben to see how much progress Ben had made.

When he arrived home would Piers go straight upstairs to his own room, or would he linger in the kitchen, perhaps even telling her something about his work? Although she was loath to admit it, Georgia had actually missed him in his absence. On more occasions than were reasonable she had caught herself looking upwards to the top-storey windows when she was out in the garden working with Ben, as though she was hoping she might catch a glimpse of Piers standing there.

It was just because the house was so large and she was on her own that she felt a little anxious about being there, she reassured herself as she drove home. That was all!

'I'm off now,' Piers told his partner, briefly popping his head round Jason's office door.

'Mmm… Thanks for sorting out that problem for me,' Jason told him. 'Sorry to drag you away from your house-hunting. Have you found anything suitable yet, by the way?'

'I've got the details of a couple of hopefuls,' Piers told him cautiously.

He had, in fact, made appointments to discuss both

properties later in the afternoon with the agents, prior to making appointments to view them, which was why he was so anxious to leave the city and drive back to Wrexford. Both properties were large and set in extensive grounds. One of them was a modern home, purpose-built by an architect for contemporary living, whilst the other was a large Georgian farmhouse set in several acres of land and badly in need of restoration.

Common sense suggested that the modern property would be the one to go for, but Piers couldn't get out of his mind a mental image of Georgia's face if she were asked to choose between the two properties. There was no doubt which one she would go for. The farmhouse just cried out to be filled with a happy tumble of children and pets, and there was certainly enough scope within the existing muddle of neglected rooms to convert one of them into a large, welcoming, family-sized kitchen, complete with flagged floors and a heartwarming Aga.

Flagged floors! Agas! Children! Pets! Since when had any of those been on *his* particular priority list?

What was happening to him? Why should one kiss shared with a woman whom logic told him he had absolutely nothing whatsoever in common with suddenly contaminate his plans for the future in much the same way that a bug could contaminate a computer system?

It had initially irritated him and then bemused him just how often Georgia had stolen her way into his thoughts over the last few days, appearing in them when she had no right to do so, when there was no logical or rational purpose in her being there.

On several occasions he had been on the point of telephoning her—just to check that that irresponsible hound hadn't totally wrecked his godmother's home, of course. There had been nothing personal in the impulse wilfully whispering to him that he needed to speak with her. It was just his sense of responsibility, his *duty* that had urged him to do so.

Just as it was his sense of responsibility that had urged him to return to Wrexford earlier than he had planned and to view a property which rationally he knew was totally unsuitable for his purposes.

Older property always sold well, though, he argued with himself. Prospective buyers fell in love with the notion of a traditional country farmhouse and a traditional country lifestyle. And so, mentally, Piers rationalised his decision to view a property which intellectually he knew filled none of the criteria he had drawn up for his house purchase.

By rights Georgia had no place in his thoughts at all other than as the scheming young woman who had palmed Ben off on his unsuspecting godmother. By rights he had every reason to feel suspicious and wary of her, and that, of course, was really why he had cut short his time in the city to return to Wrexford. His decision was in no way whatsoever connected with those vivid mental flashes he had had of Georgia's tousled curls and her violet-blue eyes, nor with the innocent sensuality of the arousal he had seen so openly expressed in the shocked darkness of those eyes after he had kissed her. No way at all… Not one tiny little bit…

The very idea of repeating that unplanned kiss was a complete anathema to him, and as for those other and far more intimate thoughts and desires which had somehow or other wormed their way into his subconscious— well, they were most definitely not anything he had any wish whatsoever to pursue—ever—either in the mental

privacy of his own thoughts or the physical privacy of
his bedroom.

'Good boy...oh, *good* dog, Ben,' Georgia praised enthusiastically as Ben obligingly sat on command.

They were on their way back from a long walk along
the river and then through some fields, following the
well-marked footpath. Now, though, it was time to get
down to some serious work, and as they got within sight
of Mrs Latham's Georgia told herself happily that Ben
was quite definitely showing signs of improvement.

Next week she had actually booked herself off some
days' leave so that she could spend even more time
working with him, and now, as she paused to bend down
and stroke him and praise him a third time, she was
beginning to feel increasingly optimistic about the outcome of the challenge she had accepted.

Happily anticipating the moment when Piers would
have to eat humble pie and Ben would reveal himself
to be a perfectly trained and obedient dog, Georgia was
unaware of the geese who had decided to land on the
large pool the river formed in front of the house, just as
she was also unaware of the sleek dark maroon Jaguar
that belonged to Piers, or the fact that Piers was driving
towards her.

The first intimation she had of impending disaster was
when Ben suddenly took off, jerking so hard on his lead
that she was tugged with him, completely missing her
footing as she tried to pull him back, mistaking the
boggy edges of the river bank for solid ground and then
gasping out loud in shock as the earth gave way beneath
her and she tumbled into the river after Ben.

The geese who had unwittingly precipitated Ben's
flight took off in a flurry of wings and noisy honks

whilst Georgia, standing almost knee-deep in the water, made an anxious grab for Ben's lead as he attempted to swim after the geese, but missed it and had to resort to paddling into the river after him. To her relief, once he realised the geese had actually gone he stopped, giving Georgia a commiserating doggy smile as she caught up with him, as though he assumed that she was as disappointed that the fowl had escaped as he was himself.

'Oh, Ben,' Georgia protested ruefully.

Both of them were soaking wet, but she expected that Ben looked far better than she did.

Wearily she fished for his lead, and then, having found it, firmly marched him towards the bank.

As Ben scrambled on to dry land and she followed suit the first thing to catch Georgia's eye was the immaculate car parked only yards away.

A horrible sense of doom sat unpleasantly in her stomach. That car was Piers's and there was Piers himself, getting out of the driver's seat and walking determinedly towards them.

'Ben,' Georgia called out frantically, but it was too late. Ben too had seen Piers, and recognised him.

Georgia winced as she saw the wet dog launch himself enthusiastically towards Piers. She couldn't bear to look—couldn't bear to see the effect of so many pounds of wet, muddy dog on Piers's immaculate person. Despairingly she waited for Piers's vocal fury, but then when she heard nothing other than a very stern, 'Sit,' she opened her eyes warily and saw, to her astonishment, that Ben was sitting obediently a yard away from Piers, watching him. Georgia had to admit that Piers was made of stern stuff as he didn't hesitate to take hold of the wet, slimy lead, his mouth hardening to a wry grimace as he studied the even wetter dog, but the expression in his eyes was nothing to the one she could see there when he finally turned his head in *her* direction.

For a moment Georgia almost expected him to repeat the command to her that he had just given to the dog. Then the nippy little wind that seemed to have sprung up out of nowhere brushed her water-chilled body and she gave a small convulsive shudder, her teeth starting to chatter, and Piers said abruptly,

'Inside...'

'It wasn't Ben's fault...' Georgia started to tell him in between shivers as she had to half run to catch up with his long strides as they headed for the house. 'He'd been behaving beautifully, and—'

'Beautifully?' Piers swung round as he started to unlock the door and stated grimly, 'He damn nearly drowned you and—'

'No! It was an accident; he just caught me off guard...' Georgia protested.

'And if it had been my *godmother* he had caught off guard?' Piers demanded flatly as he pushed open the door.

Georgia bit her lip. Piers did have a point.

'Upstairs and into a hot bath,' Piers told her curtly.

'I don't...' Georgia began, fully intending to tell him that she wasn't a child and that she didn't need him to tell her what she ought to do, but then she had to stop as she felt a huge sneeze overwhelming her, and she could see from the expression in Piers's eyes that he wasn't going to listen to any arguments. Besides, the thought of a delicious warm bath chasing the icy chills from her cold body was too tempting to resist. Even so...

'Ben needs drying...' she said, but Piers shook his head.

'I'll deal with Ben,' he told her grimly.

For a moment Georgia hesitated. Ben was soaking wet and needed rubbing dry, and he hadn't had his evening meal as yet, but then another huge sneeze overwhelmed her, at the same time as Piers took what almost looked like a small, threatening step towards her, and instinct took over. She was in the hallway and halfway up the stairs before she knew it.

In the kitchen Piers found the towels that his godmother used for just such a purpose to briskly rub Ben dry. The dog quite happily stood still whilst Piers dried him, even, a little to Piers's surprise, obligingly lifting his paws so that they too could have the river mud removed from them.

In fact, as Piers was forced to admit, Ben's manners whilst Piers performed these unplanned chores was nothing short of exemplary, even to the extent of going immediately and obediently to his bed when Piers commanded him to and waiting there patiently whilst Piers prepared his food.

Was it a coincidence or had Georgia made far more progress with the dog's training than Piers had anticipated?

Georgia! Piers's mouth tightened into a stern line as he recollected the moment when he had seen her being dragged into the river. Despite the fact that he knew perfectly well that it was safely shallow at that point, Piers had had to resist a serious urge to go in after her, but whether or not that urge had been caused by a desire to rescue her or a strong temptation to drown her, he didn't know. More likely drown her, Piers told himself irritably. He had never known anyone cause such havoc in his life before. It was becoming increasingly obvious to him that wherever Georgia and Ben went trouble automatically seemed to follow, but that *didn't* mean that he had to be on hand to rescue them or protect them. Why should he?

Ben was his godmother's dog, he reminded himself immediately. He had promised her that he would look after him for her, and if looking after him meant that he also had to look after the irritating young woman who had dared to challenge his determination to remove Ben from his godmother's life, then so be it. And it was absolutely totally impossible for him to have any kind of hidden motivation or secret subconscious agenda for his decision to bring Georgia closer into his own orbit.

Having her living here in the house with him had been a totally logical decision—given all the circumstances. True, it might have been a little foolish of him to allow her to provoke him into giving her the opportunity to prove him wrong about Ben—not that there was any possibility that she *could* do so. It was obvious to anyone that the dog was a totally unsuitable pet for his godmother. No, it had simply been his fairmindedness that had forced him to at least give her the opportunity to prove him wrong. That was all. That was totally and completely all, and, of course, it *wouldn't* have made any difference whatsoever to his decision had she been a different type of woman...

Piers frowned as he realised how long Georgia had been upstairs and how quiet it was. She had been shivering when they'd come inside, quite plainly suffering from cold and shock. Frowning even more fiercely Piers filled the kettle.

It wasn't *his* duty to look after her. She wasn't *his* responsibility. The kettle was starting to boil; swiftly he spooned coffee into a mug and added a generous spoonful of sugar.

* * *

Never had a bath felt so welcome and restorative, Georgia felt sure as she lay floating blissfully in the piping-hot water. She had washed her hair under the shower and also rinsed off the worst of the river water, but the temptation to soothe her chilly body in the warm water of a deep-filled bath had proved too tempting to resist—as had her impulse to add a few drops of her favourite relaxing aromatherapy oil.

Now its heavenly scent mingled with the warm, steamy atmosphere of the bathroom, totally releasing all the tension from her body...her body, but not her thoughts, she acknowledged as she reflected ruefully on the unwelcome outcome to her evening's training session with Ben. And he had been doing so well too. If it hadn't been for those wretched geese...

Georgia sighed and closed her eyes, trying to recapture her earlier mood of delicious relaxation, but it was no use. Sooner or later she was going to have to go downstairs to face Piers. What a sight she must have looked as she'd dragged herself out of the river. No wonder he had looked so angrily at her, his eyes, she was sure, filled with an expression of contemptuous disdain.

Reluctantly she stepped out of the bath and reached for the towel, wrapping it sarong-wise around her body. Then she realised she had neglected to bring her robe into the bathroom with her.

Securing her damp curls on top of her head with a tortoiseshell clip, she opened the bathroom door and stepped into the bedroom just at the same time as Piers, unable to get any response to either his brief knock on her bedroom door or to calling her name, anxiously pushed open the door and walked into the room.

As she stared at Piers Georgia wasn't aware of the way she instinctively crossed her hands over her towel-covered breasts, but Piers was, his mouth twisting a little sardonically as he wondered what she would say if he told her that, far from protecting her, her action had actually done more to focus his attention on her body and communicate to him—as though he hadn't already been aware of it—the fact that her insecurely wrapped towel was the only thing covering her naked body...

'I've brought you a cup of coffee,' he told her shortly, disliking the direction his own thoughts were taking almost as much as, he told himself, he disliked Georgia herself.

'Er...thank you...' Georgia husked, looking round frantically for somewhere to put it which would keep a seriously safe distance between them. Not that she actually felt she had anything to fear from him. Of course she didn't. She knew that, and she was certainly not going to fling herself headlong into his arms—was she? So why had it become so overwhelmingly necessary not to allow herself to get too close to him? Just because there had been that shockingly sensual moment between them when he had kissed her and she had reacted... wanted... Well, that didn't mean that she was automatically going to...that she wanted him to...that anything like that was ever going to happen between them again, Georgia reassured herself quickly.

Even so, she couldn't prevent the sharp shiver of sensation that memory evoked, causing a delicious and dangerous quiver of excitement to run through her body. She trembled openly in the grip of it, and a small soft sound of protest strangled beneath her breath as her face flushed with guilty colour at what she was thinking.

Piers, completely unaware of what was running through her mind, saw the shudder and the flush and totally misinterpreted them as signs that Georgia had suffered much more than a mere wetting and an embarrassing loss of face during her unplanned 'paddle' in the river. Quickly looking for somewhere to put down her coffee so that he could insist, physically if necessary, that she get straight into bed and stay there until he could find some means of checking her temperature, he realised that the only place for it was on the bedside table, just a few inches from where Georgia herself was standing.

Transfixed, Georgia stood there, her arms still wrapped around her body, as Piers came towards her, putting down the coffee mug before commanding, 'Bed...now...'

'Bed...?' Georgia's mobile features betrayed her, illuminating what she was thinking, shock turning her already pink face crimson and driving a warm tide of colour up over her body, her eyes widening and darkening as she looked helplessly from Piers's determined face to the bed and then back to him again.

She had heard stories from other young women of men who were sexually masterful, but to be ordered into bed like that...as though...

As he saw the expression in her eyes, and realised just what she was thinking, Piers cursed silently under his breath.

'You're shivering; you might have caught a chill. I just wanted...' he began, but as he spoke he involuntarily moved closer to her.

Georgia immediately stepped back from him, protesting shakily, 'No, *don't* come any closer.' But as she lifted her hand from her body to ward him off she inadvertently stepped back on to the hem of her big towel.

Only loosely secured around her body, and without the added security of her crossed hands, and aided in loosening further by being trapped by her foot, the towel unwrapped itself from her body.

Immediately Georgia made a despairing grab for it, and just as immediately Piers launched himself across the gap that separated them, every instinct propelling him to do the gentlemanly thing and protect her modesty. The towel, though, and perhaps fate, too, had other ideas, so that all Georgia's hands encountered was empty air whilst Piers's were unexpectedly and explosively filled with warm, silky, damp-fleshed woman.

'Oh!' Georgia's little squeak of protest somehow or other became a soft gasp that sounded much more like an invitation as she felt Piers's hands grazing her arms and then her breasts, both her towel and her initial rejection of him forgotten as her body reacted to his as though it had suddenly been filled with liquid pleasure.

As he heard her 'Oh!' change to a soft 'Mmm...' Piers reacted instinctively, wrapping his arms around her.

'I'm wet...your clothes...' Georgia managed to protest, but to tell the truth the dampening effect of her naked skin against Piers's clothes was really the last thing on her mind as her body, apparently of its own accord, nestled itself alluringly into the deliciously warm protection of Piers's embrace.

'Mmm...' she repeated on an even more breathless note as Piers's mouth came down over her own. Perhaps, she decided dizzily, he thought she needed a little extra help with her breathing, and obligingly she opened her mouth beneath his in order to assist him.

'Mmm...'

This time when he felt the shiver run through her body Piers did not make the error of mistaking it for a shiver of cold, but he still tightened his hold on her,

wrapping her even more closely against his own body—
no doubt trying to warm her, Georgia assured herself.
And since he was being so helpful and such a good
Samaritan the least she could do was to facilitate all that
he was doing to assist her.

Obviously it would be much easier for him to keep
her warm with his own body heat if she wrapped her
arms around him, and she could quite understand why
it was necessary for him to run his hands up and down
the length of her naked back. Their touch was deliciously warm—and the things it did to her spine and
her nerve-endings…! Heavens, she had had no idea that
her flesh could be so extraordinarily sensitive, and if the
way he was kissing that small, pulsing cord in the side
of her neck was perhaps just a little unorthodox, well,
it was still having the most deliciously pleasurable effect
on her senses, which surely was far more restorative
than had he adopted a more traditional means of warm-
ing her—such as proffering a hot-water bottle or a
heated blanket.

Thinking of hot-water bottles and heated blankets in-
explicably reminded Georgia of the fact that the bed was
right there, only inches away from them, and inexpli-
cably she had the oddest need to lie down on it. Probably because she was feeling so light-headed and weak,
she told herself.

Through the fine softness of Piers's shirt Georgia
could feel the heavenly warmth of his chest, and when
she opened her eyes she could see the soft darkness of
his body hair. A thrill of sensation ran right through her,
a shocking female awareness of Piers's maleness; her
fingers itched to stroke their way through that inviting
silkiness and to explore the flesh that lay beneath it. A
hundred unfamiliar and highly erotic impulses flashed

their tantalising messages to Georgia's senses, flattening immediately the tentative and semi-shocked resistance her brain put up to the wantonness of such thoughts.

Weakly Georgia told herself that it was the very unfamiliarity of such thoughts that made her feel so vulnerable towards them, so unable to deny or reject their provocative allure. The temptation to unfasten just one of the buttons on Piers's shirt, just to see if actually touching him would prove to be as deliciously erotic as she imagined, was proving impossible to resist. Just one button, she promised herself, that was all, but as her mouth meshed with Piers's responding to and returning the increasing passion of his kiss, 'just one' became two, and then three, and then, before she knew it, Piers was murmuring to her that he wanted her to take his shirt off completely. What was more, he was helping her to do so. And then, blissfully, the hard, naked warmth of his upper body was hers to touch and explore.

Vaguely Georgia was aware of how odd it was that she should want to touch Piers like this when she had never once felt even remotely tempted to explore or caress her first lover in the same almost frenziedly hungry way, but she dismissed the thought as an unnecessary and unwanted distraction from what she was doing. The silky arrowing of Piers's hair ran right down the centre of his chest—and lower—and Georgia's fingertips followed it all the way to where his belt obstructed her progress.

She heard Piers catch his breath as she stopped, lifting his mouth from hers whilst he looked deep into her eyes.

Georgia held her breath, conscious of the solemnity of the moment, and then, as Piers lifted his hand to touch her face, she saw his gaze drop to her naked breasts and stay there.

Very gently he reached out and touched her, his fingertips just stroking the merest feathering of touches along the outer curve of her breast.

Immediately Georgia gave an involuntary shiver of sensual reaction, her nipples thrusting eagerly into dark, excited peaks. Just the thought of Piers's hands cupping her naked breasts made her shudder voluptuously, but when he did so the pleasure she had imagined came nowhere near matching the real thing, and Georgia made a small soft sound of pleasure as he started to caress her.

When he picked her up and laid her gently on the bed she watched him, liquid-eyed, whilst he leaned over her, silently spanning her small waist with his hands before lifting his head to look into her eyes.

He wanted to touch and memorise every delicious curve of her, Piers decided as he felt the tiny responsive nerves jumping beneath Georgia's skin. Just the sight and scent of her aroused him to the point where... And as for that soft, liquid, melting look he could see in her eyes...

Reaching for her hand, he took hold of it in his and lifted it palm upwards to his mouth, slowly kissing the sensitive flesh of her palm and watching her reaction darken her eyes at the same time as he felt the responsive shudder go though her. And then, still holding her hand, he placed it on the fastening of his belt, holding it there as he leaned over and slowly kissed first her mouth, and then the dark points of each breast in turn, once, and then a second time and then a third.

As she felt Piers's mouth caressing her nipples Georgia cried out softly, unable to control her response, her fingers curling into the buckle of his belt. His hand was caressing the bare flesh of her hip and Georgia could feel the tiny quivers of sensation running like quicksilver inside her body, starting to gather, to coalesce, into a torrent which she knew instinctively would totally sweep her away.

Piers was drawing her nipple deeper into his mouth, and the shivers of pleasure his caress was causing her were turning into deep, fierce shudders of female reaction.

As Piers released her nipple from the sensual captivity of his mouth and tongue, feeding its hunger with the pliant caress of his fingertips, he whispered thickly to her, 'Undress me, Georgia. I want—'

'Woof!'

Both of them froze as Ben suddenly came into the room and gave one firm bark.

Ben!

Guiltily Georgia pushed Piers away. How on earth could she have forgotten not just the dog but her entire sense of reality as well?

Equally swiftly Piers moved back from Georgia. Just what the hell was he doing? Every instinct he possessed told him that Georgia was quite definitely a serious commitment type of woman. Georgia had already managed to worm not just her way, but also that of that wretched dog as well, into his godmother's affections, and now here she was, performing an equally dangerous trick on his own emotions.

'Ben!' Georgia exclaimed at the same time as Piers instructed sharply, 'Downstairs...now...'

Placidly Ben wagged his tail and headed towards the open bedroom door, but once there he simply sat down and looked at Piers.

Angrily Piers glowered at him as he got up off the bed and picked up his shirt, pulling it on before walking towards Ben. If he hadn't been far too sensible to think anything so foolish he might almost have imagined that the dog had come upstairs with the deliberate intention of interrupting them, and that he was making it equally plain that there was no way he was going to go back downstairs and leave Piers alone with Georgia.

Georgia, meanwhile, as soon as Piers had got up off the bed, had reached for her robe and pulled it on.

What on earth had come over her? There was no rational explanation for what she had done—or for what she had wanted to do.

Some hours later, on his way to bed, having checked that all the doors and windows were locked and the alarm was on, Piers paused outside Georgia's bedroom door. It was all very well for her to have claimed earlier that she wasn't suffering any after-effects from her wetting; he still...

His hand was on the door handle when Ben suddenly came padding upstairs and very determinedly lay down outside Georgia's bedroom door. *Was* it just his imagination or was the dog really looking at him, not just reproachfully but almost a little reprovingly? It *was* his imagination, of course, Piers assured himself, just as the only logical reason that Ben had come upstairs was not really to guard Georgia but simply to try and get a more comfortable bed to sleep on than the one he was officially allocated downstairs in the kitchen.

Nevertheless, Piers didn't make any attempt to return Ben to the kitchen—or to open Georgia's bedroom door.

CHAPTER FIVE

'BEN!'

Georgia tensed as she heard the wrathful warning in Piers's voice as he called Ben's name.

She had spent the whole of the previous day, her first day's leave, working with the English setter, and she had been very pleased with the results.

Ben wanted to learn, to please, but he was an energetic dog who got easily bored. Now, as she saw the way his ears went down and he looked anxiously at her before going under the table to hide as he, like her, recognised the anger in Piers's voice, all Georgia's protective instincts came to the fore.

She had been keeping as much distance as she could between her and Piers since the night of her ignominious fall into the river. After Ben had interrupted them and Piers had gone to take him downstairs Georgia had forced herself to look closely and analytically at what had happened between them, and she hadn't liked the conclusions she had had to reach.

Piers was a man, and men thought about, felt about, reacted differently to sexual intimacy than women did. Men's sexual responses did not need to be touched, coloured or enhanced by their emotions. Men, by their very natures, tended to seize the sexual moment. Who knew *what* interpretation Piers had put on her own behaviour? Heavens, he might even have thought that she had deliberately allowed her towel to slip from her grasp—he was cynical enough, worldly enough; Georgia was sure of that.

It wasn't that she felt that he had deliberately set out to seduce her; she wasn't so naive nor so melodramatic. No, she felt sure his primary intention had simply been to bring her a hot drink and to check that she was all right. Maybe, too, he had welcomed the opportunity to reinforce to her his views on Ben's behaviour; but that was all.

No, she couldn't blame him. Not entirely. *She* could have resisted, protested, withdrawn from him, but instead she had—

It had taken every ounce of courage she possessed for her to say to him the next day, 'About last night... I...it... It was a mistake,' she had told him firmly, unable to lift her gaze to meet his, as she'd walked into the kitchen and found him engaged in making his breakfast. 'It shouldn't have happened and I don't—'

'I couldn't agree more.' Piers had cut her off in a clipped voice.

As he'd leant across the table Georgia had been able to see where the sunlight left a soft gold trail on his bare forearm, and she'd had the most ridiculous urge to reach out and touch him there.

Speedily she had looked away from him, uncomfortably aware of how fast her heart was beating.

Nothing further had been said about the incident in her bedroom by either of them, and Georgia had told herself that she was glad. And certainly she was equally glad that Piers had neither said nor done anything that in any way remotely suggested it was an experience he wished to repeat.

Since then, though, she had taken great care to keep away from the kitchen when she knew that Piers was using it, and she suspected that he was doing the same thing. This morning, however, she had woken up earlier and had taken Ben for a short walk before returning to make her breakfast, only to find that Piers was in the kitchen making himself a cup of coffee, wearing only a towelling robe, his face unshaven and his hair ruffled. For some odd reason the knowledge that he had only just got out of bed had had a dangerous emotional effect on her.

She hadn't realised how much her expression was giving away until she'd heard him saying ruefully as he stroked his hand across his unshaven jaw, 'Yes, I do need a shave, but I was up half the night working.'

'Mmm…I suppose if you were married you'd have to shave at night,' she began absently, and then stopped as she realised the direction her thoughts were taking. But it was too late because Piers had already picked up on what she was thinking.

'At night—and in the morning,' he told her meaningfully, his gaze sliding from her eyes to her mouth and then back to her eyes again, so that he could enjoy the confusion he could see so clearly registered there. What *was* it about her, he wondered, that made it so impossible for him not to give in to the temptation to underline his male sexuality to her and to watch her own female reaction to his provocation?

'Stop looking at me like that,' Georgia was unable to stop herself from begging him huskily.

'Like what?' Piers teased, his gaze deliberately dropping from her mouth to her body.

'Like…like that!' Georgia protested, immediately refocusing Piers's attention on her softly parted lips.

What would she do, he wondered, if he went to her now and took her in his arms? If he kissed her? She'd

probably complain that his unshaven beard was scratching her tender skin, Piers told himself grittily, deliberately turning away from the temptation she represented
and heading for the hallway.

That had been when Georgia had heard him call out
angrily for Ben.

'What's wrong?' she enquired now, following Piers
into the hall and then stopping as she saw the shredded
copy of his morning paper.

'Oh!'

'Oh, indeed,' Piers agreed grimly.

'It's only a newspaper.' Georgia defended the dog.
'It won't take two minutes for me to go out and get you
another one.'

'That's not the point,' Piers told her sharply. 'Don't
think I don't know why you're so determined to keep
him here,' he told Georgia grimly. 'After all, *you* were
the one who pressurised my godmother into having him
in the first place.'

'I did no such thing,' Georgia immediately retorted
indignantly.

'No? That's not the way my godmother tells it,' Piers
contradicted her flatly. 'According to her, it's *you* she
has to thank for having Ben.'

'Oh, but that's...' Georgia began, intending to tell
him that it was because of her absence from the waiting
room that his previous owner had managed to persuade
his godmother into becoming Ben's new owner.

But Piers was in no mood to listen, overruling her
before she had any chance to finish what she was saying,
telling her curtly, 'I should have thought that your pro-
fessionalism alone would have made you think twice
about putting emotional pressure on my godmother to
take Ben on. Suggesting that he might have to be put

to sleep if she didn't have him was, in my view, a serious breach of professional conduct, and—'

'I never told Mrs Latham any such thing,' Georgia gasped.

'Perhaps not in so many words,' Piers allowed. 'But you certainly gave her the impression that that's what would have happened to him.'

As the sound of their raised voices reached Ben through the half-open kitchen door he put his nose on his paws and listened anxiously to them. Human beings! They could be so hard to understand at times.

Piers frowned as he pulled up in front of the house he had come to view. From the details he had received on it he had decided that it sounded ideal for his purposes. Modern, architect-designed, spacious, with a good-sized garden to ensure his privacy—it even had a room specifically designed to house computer equipment.

The selling agent who was due to meet him here had extolled its virtues to Piers when he had initially expressed an interest in it, adding helpfully that because the property was already empty Piers could move into it virtually as soon as he wished.

Yes, this property was almost perfectly suited to his needs, unlike the farmhouse which was the only other remotely suitable property the agent had had on his books.

As he had pondered before, there was no doubt whatsoever in his mind that Georgia would go for the farmhouse. She would probably insist on raising a brood of chickens, which she would want to have wandering about in the farmyard, and no doubt she would want to turn at least one of the outbuildings into temporary accommodation for all the animal waifs and strays she would insist on adopting. He would be lucky if he didn't find himself financing a donkey sanctuary, as well as providing a refuge for wild, untrainable dogs, and their children would probably grow up to be as animal-mad as their mother, so that his would be the only lone voice of sanity and restraint in the entire household.

Not that both she and their children wouldn't do their very best to subvert his desire to keep their lives as animal-free as possible. He could see it now: the lone school hamster who was brought home 'for the holidays' and who never went back; the stray cat who made her home with them and unexpectedly produced a litter of kittens; the pony his daughter would insist on having—and he would, of course, give in.

'But she'll have to clean it and feed it herself, I'm not getting up at the crack of dawn every day to do it...'

To his consternation Piers realised that he had not only spoken his thoughts out loud but that, for one moment, his imagination had produced such an intensely real mental picture for him that it was as though his imaginary daughter was actually here, standing in front of him, her mother's dark red curls bouncing with determination as she besieged him with pleas and entreaties.

Her mother's red hair... Georgia's red hair... But he wasn't...he didn't... The clanking of the automatic wrought-iron gates opening alerted him to the estate agent's arrival, bringing a thankful end to his disturbing thoughts.

'It would be the perfect property for a man in your position,' the agent enthused as they finished viewing the house and he locked the front door. 'It fulfils all the criteria you gave us.'

'Yes,' Piers agreed unenthusiastically.

'It's got vacant possession, and I know that the owner is prepared to negotiate on price,' the agent persevered.

'Mmm… What time is my appointment to view the farmhouse?' Piers asked him briefly.

'The farmhouse?' The agent's smile turned to a small frown. 'I have made an appointment for you to view it,' he began cautiously, 'but I must warn you, it is in need of some quite serious renovation.'

'I imagine it must be,' Piers agreed urbanely. 'It is over two hundred years old.'

'Well, yes, and if you were wanting a period family house then…' He paused and shrugged. 'I have to warn you, though, that we already have at least one seriously interested buyer, despite the fact that its survey showed the house could be subject to serious flooding if the river was ever to rise above its banks…and…'

'Has it ever done so?' Piers asked him quietly.

'Well, no…at least not in the last hundred years,' the agent conceded. 'But, as I'm sure you'll agree once you've viewed it, it comes nowhere as near to fulfilling your specifications in the way that this property does.'

It was quite plain to Piers that the agent was trying to push him into buying the house he had just viewed, and on the face of it he knew that he had to agree with everything that the other man was saying. After all, he hadn't raised any points that Piers hadn't already seen for himself. The farmhouse was a *family* home, and, to judge from the carefully worded estate agent's blurb, in need of having a considerable amount of money spent on it, whereas the one he had just looked at needed nothing other than his own furniture. Even the floors were polished wood and didn't need carpeting. It cried out for the kind of minimalistic décor that went perfectly with the kind of business image he *ought* to want to portray.

Crumbling plasterwork and an Aga were not the right backdrop for someone who was selling himself and his skills as an expert in the writing of the most technologically advanced computer software in the marketplace. He would have to have one of the outbuildings virtually rebuilt to house all his equipment, and even then...

Abruptly Piers dragged himself back to reality. In a bygone age a man suffering from what he was suffering from might genuinely have believed that Georgia had cast some kind of spell over him. But to think that was to believe that Georgia wanted him in her life, and she had made it more than evident that she had no such desire at all.

But she did desire *him*. Or at least she had done so when...

A small, discreet cough from the estate agent reminded Piers of where he was. He wasn't going to put in an offer for the farmhouse—of course he wasn't, he assured himself as he got into his car. It just made sense to view the only property locally that could provide him with a yardstick to measure the suitability of the house he had just viewed; that was all. Of course it was.

Georgia was feeling very pleased with herself, *and* with Ben. Shortly after Piers had left she had received a telephone call from the local paper asking if they could interview her that morning about the scheme she had originated for pets and their owners to visit the old people's home. Even though Georgia had told the reporter that the idea wasn't original, and that she was simply copying a scheme already in force in several other parts of the country, she had nevertheless agreed to be interviewed.

The reporter had arrived promptly half an hour later and the interview had gone very well. Rick Siddington was quite obviously an animal lover himself, and he had quickly endeared himself, to the owners whom he was also interviewing by making a big fuss of their pets.

Georgia had diplomatically left Ben behind on this occasion, sensing that he was all too likely to try to steal the other dogs' thunder. Philip had actually come out of his office to speak with the reporter himself, and Georgia had been able to tell from the way he had smiled at her and patted her paternally on the arm that she had been forgiven her transgressions over the training class which Ben had disrupted—for the time being at least! Now, back home and having just finished grooming Ben, she sat back on her heels and surveyed his silky coat admiringly.

'Good dog, Ben,' she praised him repeatedly before giving him a small doggy treat for his good behaviour whilst she had been brushing him.

As Ben went to the door and asked to go out Georgia reflected modestly as she opened it for him that he really was making good progress, thanks just as much to his own canine intelligence as to her training skills—skills which, according to Piers, she simply did not possess. That jibe still had the power to hurt her, but nowhere near as much as the accusation he had thrown at her that she had deliberately encouraged his godmother to give Ben a home whilst knowing that he was a totally unsuitable dog for her. Those words had stung, all the more so because they simply weren't true.

How *could* he be so hateful to her so soon after he

had...after they had...? But hadn't she already warned herself that the intimacy which had left her so helplessly incapable of denying the sweetly heady sensual desire he had aroused in her, had meant nothing emotionally to him? He had probably kissed a dozen women as passionately as he had kissed her, probably more—whilst she...

A self-conscious pink wash of colour stained her skin as she remembered how she had lain there on the bed, totally naked, practically basking in the look she had seen in his eyes. That kind of behaviour was totally out of character for her, but she would be foolish to imagine that what had happened meant anything to him. If it had—

She could hear a loud angry roar through the open kitchen window. Someone was shouting at Ben.

'Come here, you—'

Anxiously Georgia ran to the kitchen door.

A smartly dressed elderly gentleman was marching up the garden path, his face red with temper.

'Is this *your* dog?' he demanded angrily.

From his bearing and his clipped voice, Georgia guessed that he was an ex-serviceman.

'Er...in a manner of speaking,' she agreed hesitantly as she studied Ben's soil-encrusted nose and paws.

'What do you mean? Either he is or he isn't,' the man snapped impatiently. 'Damn hound! Caught him digging up my vegetable garden.'

'Oh, no, I'm so sorry,' Georgia apologised immediately.

'"Sorry" won't undo the damage he's caused,' she was told acidly. 'If you own a dog you should keep him under control... He deserves to be shot.'

'Oh, no!' Georgia protested, her face paling whilst

she tried frantically to work out how on earth Ben had managed to escape from the garden, which she knew Mrs Latham had had surrounded by a special 'dog-proof' fence at considerable expense.

'I'll pay for whatever damage he's caused,' Georgia offered, inwardly hoping it wouldn't prove to be too much. She could understand the man's anger. Her own father was a very keen gardener and she knew how he would have felt if someone's dog had dug up *his* prize vegetable patch.

'Hmm... The estate agent told me when I bought my house that this was a *quiet* area, with most of the properties owned by older people...'

'Well, I don't actually *own* this house,' Georgia felt bound to explain.

'But you do own this...this *dog*?' he insisted grimly.

'I... No, Ben, no,' Georgia commanded sharply as Ben, growing bored, playfully crept up to the man and made to jump up at him, leaving a set of muddy paw-prints on his immaculate grey trousers.

'Oh, I really am sorry,' she apologised again. 'He's...he's only a young dog and he—'

'He's a menace, *that's* what he is. He ought to be chained up,' the man growled acerbically at her. 'And if I find him in my garden again he's going to wish that he was. There's a law in this country now about allowing dogs to roam.'

Guiltily Georgia listened to his tirade, knowing there was nothing she could reasonably say or do to make amends.

'Six months of hard work gone completely to waste,' the man was telling her furiously. 'You should see what he's done to my prize dahlias... I was growing them for the County Show and—'

'What's going on here?'

Neither of them had heard Piers walking into the garden, and Georgia's face went as pale as the man's was flushed as she saw him standing there.

How much had he overheard?

Just as she was about to launch into an edited explanation of what had happened the man beat her to it, turning to him and demanding furiously, 'That damn dog of yours has just ruined my garden. Caught him down by the young lettuces, digging the whole of them up. Your wife's offered to pay for the damage but that isn't the point. That dog—'

'I'm not—'

'She isn't—'

As they both spoke at once Georgia clenched one hand and stopped. Let Piers explain the situation to his godmother's angry neighbour. He would probably do a far better job of doing so than she could. But to her consternation, as Piers continued to explain to him that they were not actually married, the man jumped to the wrong conclusion and exclaimed bitingly, 'Hah! I suppose I should have known. It's all of a piece—no standards…no morals… That's what's wrong with you modern young people. In *my* day a young man took his responsibilities seriously, whether they were to a woman or to a dog, *and* he had to buy a licence for both, just to prove his good faith and his intentions to honour his responsibility to them and to the community at large. But of course it's all different now—no respect for anything or anyone…'

'Just a moment!'

Piers's voice cracked like a whip as he spoke sharply to the other man, commanding his attention and his silence.

'Whether or not a couple choose to marry is *their* business and no one else's. A man proves his respect *and* his love for the woman he commits himself to by the way he treats her and their relationship. And I can promise you that *my* responsibilities are something *I* take very seriously indeed.'

Piers moved closer to Georgia—so close to her in fact that for one wild, illogical moment she almost felt as though he had done so out of a desire to defend and protect her.

'I'm sorry.' The other man began to stutter, suddenly looking older and very much more frail than he had done when he had first arrived. He was elderly, and a little out of step with modern life, and probably, because of that, a little intimidated by it, Georgia guessed. And she could well understand how angry Ben's destruction of his garden must have made him feel.

'Look, why don't you come in and have a cup of tea?' she suggested gently to him. 'Then we can discuss what can be done to put matters right.'

Georgia could see the look of surprise on Piers's face, but suddenly she felt almost sorry for the older man, sensing intuitively that he was probably rather lonely.

'I...er...'

'Yes, that's an excellent idea,' Piers agreed, smiling as he added, 'Only instead of tea perhaps a strong G and T might be more in order.'

'Well...now you're talking,' the older man agreed heartily.

In the end their unexpected visitor stayed for over an hour, and they learned that he was a retired colonel whose wife had died two years earlier, and that his decision to move to the area had been prompted by a visit he and his wife had made to the town many years earlier.

'No family, you see. Both of us only ones, so no family to speak of. Felt that it would have been what Ethel would have liked...'

'Well, I'm sure when my godmother returns she'll be very keen to introduce you to her bridge cronies,' Piers informed him.

'Bridge?' The colonel's eyes gleamed with interest. 'Haven't had much time to get involved socially as yet. The vicar called round, of course, but I'm not a church-going man, never have been. Ethel liked a good sermon...'

By the time he got up to go it was agreed that Ben's destruction of his garden was to be forgotten just so long as there wasn't a repeat performance. However, the harmonious end to the day was somewhat marred for Georgia as, when he stood on the front doorstep, the colonel turned to them both and confided, 'Shouldn't say so, perhaps, but it seems to me that a dog like that is too much of a handful for a mature lady... A little house dog would be much better...'

After he had gone Georgia waited tensely for the stinging condemnation she was sure that Piers was going to utter, but, to her surprise, as she carefully washed the heavy crystal glasses he had used for their drinks, he came up to her and told her quietly, 'That was very well done of you; he's obviously very lonely, poor chap, although I admit for a moment when he... In your shoes I doubt that I'd have had the compassion to offer him a cup of tea.'

'He was very angry,' Georgia responded, dipping her head over the hot washing-up water to conceal the shock his praise had given her.

'With good reason,' Piers told her dryly, adding, 'How did Ben get out, by the way?'

'I'm not sure. We'll have to check the fence and make sure any holes are safely mended.'

She gave a small sigh. 'I'll go round tomorrow to see the colonel. My father's a keen gardener and I know how he'd feel in the same circumstances. Perhaps something can be salvaged.'

'Now I think I begin to understand just what motivated you to persuade my godmother to take Ben on,' Piers said wryly. 'You're far too soft-hearted...'

'No, I'm not at all,' Georgia protested, turning towards him defensively. 'I can be very determined when I need to be.'

'Very determined to be a soft touch,' Piers scoffed, and then, to Georgia's astonishment, he added huskily, 'Have you *any* idea how much, right now, I want to kiss you?'

'To...to kiss me...?' Georgia stammered, her face flushing guiltily as she recognised how much she actually wanted him to put his words into action. Veiling her expression from him with downcast eyelashes, just in case he should see what she was feeling, she began huskily, 'I...I don't think that that would be a good idea...'

'You don't?'

'I...I don't know why you should. After all...'

'You don't?' Piers repeated, his voice becoming even more throaty and sexy. 'Does *this* make it any easier for you to see why?' he asked her softly as he moved towards her, the bulk of his body cutting off her escape as he placed his hands at either side of her on the worktop. The white tee shirt he was wearing revealed most of his arms, and, as she had been before, Georgia was overwhelmed by a desire to reach out and stroke her fingertips down their length. They looked so strong, so masculine…so…so sexy… so…so him.

She gave a small ecstatic sigh of feminine bliss and closed her eyes, opening them again in breathless shock as she felt the warm pressure of Piers's mouth probing the softness of her own.

'Piers…no…' she started to say, but for some reason her firm denial was voiced as a husky, 'Mmm…'

'Mmm…' Piers echoed, in a much deeper and more possessive masculine tone. 'It would be so easy to make love to you,' he told her rawly, the words pouring hotly into her ear as his hand caressed the narrow curve of her waist. 'I could take you here…now…'

'In the kitchen?' Georgia squeaked breathlessly. She wasn't used to strong gin and tonics, especially when she had only managed to eat a snacky sandwich. The liquor must have gone to her head, loosening her tongue as well as her inhibitions, she reflected as Piers seemed to interpret what she had intended to be a statement of rejection and distaste as one of curiosity and encouragement.

'Mmm…shall I show you how?' Piers asked her, and then, without waiting for her response, he was picking her up, lifting her off her feet, holding her powerfully against his body. He whispered wickedly to her, 'We could use the table. I could lay you on it and unfasten your shirt…'

Georgia could feel the heat of his gaze scorching her skin right through her clothes as he looked at her breasts, and she could feel, too, the little prickle of excitement that puckered her nipples into tight, eager points.

'And then…?' Georgia heard herself gasping huskily.

'And then I'd hold your breasts in my hands and I'd stroke and tease your nipples until you were begging for me to take them into my mouth, just as I'd be begging for you to touch and taste me,' Piers told her in a raw growl.

'And then I'd touch you here...' he told her, his hand just lightly skimming the junction of her thighs, the lightest, briefest touch imaginable, but it was enough to make her melt with longing, to burn with need and to show every bit of what she was feeling in her eyes.

'And you'd look at me...just the way you're looking at me right now,' Piers told her thickly, 'and I'd want you so much that I'd almost be afraid of hurting you, knowing that the way I wanted to have you would be hot and passionate, and it wouldn't be over for a long, long time; that I'd want to explore every inch of you... touch you...stroke you...know you...eat you...'

'Piers...' Georgia managed to protest chokily.

'Piers what?' he asked her, his fingers already sliding inside the fastening of her shirt and hooking round the buttons. 'Do you want me as much as I want you, sweet Georgia?' Piers asked her, his fingertips tantalising her as they slid sensually against her skin.

Her breasts ached so for his touch... his mouth... Georgia shivered in mute pleasure as she heard him whispering to her, 'Do you lie in bed at night thinking of me the way I think of you...imagining the soft silkiness of your skin, the sweet taste of you...that sexy little purr you make when you're aroused...?'

In another second he would be touching her nipple, and once he did... He was just toying with her, amusing himself, that was all; he didn't really feel anything for her. Right now he might say he wanted her, but tomorrow he would be behaving horribly to her again; she knew it. Frantically Georgia clung to what she knew to be reality.

'We can't,' she protested thickly. 'We don't… We're enemies, Piers,' she reminded him.

'Enemies?'

His fingers stilled on their sensual journey across her skin. Slowly he withdrew them from her body as he stood up, releasing her.

'Enemies? Is that how you see us? Yes, I suppose you're right,' he agreed curtly, and then he walked away from her, opening the kitchen door and then very quietly closing it behind him.

Georgia ached to call him back, but somehow she managed to prevent herself from doing so. As though he sensed what she was feeling, Ben climbed out of his basket and came across to lean against her. Automatically Georgia stroked his fur, wondering why it should suddenly feel so damp and then realising that she was actually crying. Crying? Over Piers? What a fool she was being. The next thing she knew she would be thinking she had fallen in love with him! And she was far too sensible to allow anything like *that* to happen. Far too sensible!

CHAPTER SIX

IT HAD never been destined to be recorded as one of the best days of his life right from the start, Piers was to acknowledge grimly, twenty-four hours after the event which was to change his life for ever.

For a start he did something he could never remember having done before. He overslept. He *never* overslept. Never. But this morning he had done, waking up abruptly with the beginnings of what promised to be a bad headache and an even worse mood.

And it didn't make him feel any better to be forced to acknowledge that at least part of the cause of his mood was the fact that in his dreams his desire for Georgia had given him such an ache of longing for her that on waking he'd actually felt as though she had physically been there in bed with him, deliberately arousing him and then withdrawing from him, teasing him, tormenting him with the alluring promise of her softly naked body whilst, at the same time, refusing to allow him to touch her.

Angrily he pushed back the bedcovers. Lying in bed mentally going over his dreams wasn't going to do anything to change them, or the message they were no doubt trying to give him.

Scowling, he headed for his bathroom.

Georgia wasn't having a much better day. During his walk Ben had run off, dancing around her just out of her reach whilst she alternately tried to coax and order

him back to her. In the end it had only been with the
aid of a fellow walker whose pretty sheltie bitch Ben
had taken a shine to that she had managed to get his
lead back on him.

Back at the house she had fed him, and answered a
telephone call from work concerning the disappearance
of some papers she knew for a fact she had given to the
office manager to be filed.

Now, as she concluded her telephone call, she realised that Ben was nowhere in sight—just like Piers, who
presumably had got up early and left the house before
she had come down.

His comments, his behaviour towards her had left her
not just aching with longing for him but having to con-
front as well the reasons why she was reacting to him
the way she was, the reasons she wanted him the way
she did.

She was just reassuring herself for the hundred and
somethingth time that she most certainly was *not* in love
with him when she heard his furious shout, followed, as
she rushed to open the kitchen door, by a far less noisy
but far more ominous deeply angry call of, "Ben". This
shouting after Ben was coming to be a habit.

As she rushed to the stairs, her heart pounding nervously, Georgia stopped dead.

Ben was on his way downstairs, and in his mouth…

She swallowed and closed her eyes in dismay, praying that the shoe—that very mangled and chewed shoe
Ben was so proudly bringing to her, his whole body
wriggling with happy excitement—did not belong to
Piers, even though she could see quite clearly that it
was most definitely a man's shoe, and the only man in
the house was Piers.

As Ben dutifully dropped the shoe at her feet and then

stood back, waiting for her to praise him, Georgia's heart sank even further. She had been throwing sticks for him when she'd walked him, praising him for returning to her with them, and now...

As she looked up the stairs she could see Piers walking slowly down, watching them both.

'This is your handiwork, I suppose,' he accused her menacingly.

'I... He...' Georgia fell silent, then shook her head as she told Ben sorrowfully, 'Bad dog, Ben.'

The dog's tail dropped, and so did his nose, his eyes losing their expectant shine. Georgia could feel a huge lump forming in her throat as she forgot what an archmanipulator Ben could be and remembered only that the dog was probably simply carrying out a ritual she herself had taught him.

'That dog—' Piers began, but Georgia, fearing what he might say, immediately leapt to Ben's defence.

She told him quickly, 'He wasn't being deliberately destructive. He's simply following his instincts of retrieval.'

'With *my* shoe?' Piers asked her sarcastically.

'It's because he relates to you as a member of his pack.' Georgia defended the dog. 'And he—'

'Those shoes are—*were*—leather and handmade,' Piers overrode her coldly.

Handmade leather shoes. Georgia's heart sank even further. She could just imagine how much they would cost to replace, and, of course, she would have to offer to replace them, although technically Ben wasn't her dog.

'I'll pay to replace them, of course,' she offered quickly.

'They're handmade,' Piers repeated. 'That means

they take time to be made. One can't simply go out and just *buy* a pair...'

He really was enjoying making her squirm, Georgia decided, anger starting to replace her initial feelings of dismay and guilt.

'Ben obviously shares your expensive tastes,' she told him lightly. 'But I'm sure they can't be the *only* pair of shoes you possess.'

The dull ache in his head which Piers had woken up with had turned with unpleasant speed into the kind of headache he knew, from past experience, would quickly reach a raging crescendo of pain unless he took something for it...and soon. It infuriated him that instead of castigating the dog Georgia actually seemed to be defending him, and even implying that *he*, Piers, *deserved* to have his shoes destroyed. He hadn't missed either that faintly scornful look in her eyes when he had pointed out to her that the shoes were handmade and expensive. Perhaps he *had* sounded like the worst kind of successful entrepreneur, but he hadn't intended to be boastful—simply to make her understand the gravity of Ben's crime.

'No,' he agreed, now suddenly as defensive over his choice of footwear as Georgia had been over Ben's enjoyment of it. 'They aren't the only pair I have to wear, but right at this moment they are the only pair I wanted to wear, the pair I had chosen to wear. Not that it matters. The real issue here is—'

Ben, not getting the reaction he had hoped for from Georgia, darted forward and picked up the shoe, proudly carrying it right to Georgia's feet and sitting down waiting for her to praise him. Helplessly Georgia looked from the dog's expectant eyes to Piers's condemning ones.

'He isn't being deliberately destructive,' she repeated to Piers helplessly. 'He thinks…he believes…' She stopped as she saw the way Piers's mouth was curling with biting anger.

'Perhaps you were right after all… Perhaps he *is* far more intelligent, far easier to train than I believed,' Piers told her with deliberation, sharply biting off each word as he delivered them to her almost like condemnatory blows.

'I haven't taught him to do that,' Georgia retorted hotly as the meaning of what Piers had said sank in. 'I throw sticks for him to retrieve…like any other dog owner, but as to shoes…'

She stopped, unable to hold the silent contempt of the look he was giving her, his eyes smouldering darkly with the dislike he so obviously felt for her in the angry whiteness of his face.

The pain in his head had reached a crashing crescendo, Piers recognised. It infuriated him more than he wanted to admit, even to himself, that Georgia should choose the dog above him; that she should defend Ben so determinedly, so tenderly and lovingly, even though she must know that *he* was right. And what made it worse was that he suspected that had the shoe Ben had chewed belonged to anyone else other than him she would have taken a completely different stance.

'You're enjoying this, aren't you?' he accused her furiously.

'Enjoying it!' The unjustness of his accusation caused Georgia to retaliate immediately. 'No, I am not.'

'Well, you'd better make the most of it,' Piers advised her as waves of nauseating pain began to lash the inside of his head. 'Because you're not going to find the situation anything like so funny when I present you with the bill for my shoes, and even less so when you explain to my godmother how *your* claims to be able to train her dog have resulted in him displaying the kind of antisocial behaviour that just confirms that he needs to be found a new owner—preferably one who *doesn't* wear shoes,' he finished savagely.

Now Georgia's face was as white as Piers's and her pain nearly as great as well, although hers was located in her heart rather than in her head.

'It isn't up to *you* to say whether Ben stays or goes,' she reminded him protectively.

'No,' Piers said softly, with such a vitriolic look that Georgia caught her breath in alarm, immediately moving closer to Ben and putting her hand protectively on his collar.

'If you try to do *anything* to hurt or harm Ben...' she began warningly, and then stopped as she saw the look that zigzagged briefly through Piers's eyes, her breath catching in her throat. Pain... Piers had felt pain, had looked betrayed. Pain! But how could that be? Surely that meant...? But before she could follow up her intriguing line of thought Piers was turning away from her and heading back up the stairs to his own part of the house.

As he took the tablets he knew would help the pain of his headache to subside, Piers cursed himself for his lack of self-control. Jealous of a dog... What the hell was happening to him? He closed his eyes and tried to breathe slowly and deeply, telling himself he was doing so simply to speed up the progress of the drug through his system, but in reality he knew there was more to it than that...much more...

To his intense irritation, behind his closed eyelids all

he could see was Georgia's anguished face as she looked protectively towards Ben. Perhaps he *had* over-reacted a little—but what man in love could calmly or rationally accept that the woman he loved cared more about a dog than she did about him?

A man in love!

Since when had *he* been *that*? He wasn't inhuman. He had nothing against people falling in love. Love was a very wonderful and special thing. It was just that, for some reason, he hadn't imagined it happening to him. Or, rather, he hadn't imagined it happening to him in quite the fashion that it had. He had assumed that when love finally entered his life it—*she* would enter it calmly, in a dignified mature fashion. Not sweep in in a whirlwind of complex, volatile, *challenging* emotions that went from one extreme to the other and then back again in the space of a heartbeat. And certainly never, ever had he imagined that he would be competing for his beloved's affections with a dog!

The tablets he had taken were starting to do their work, easing the pain out of his head. A glance at his watch revealed the unwelcome fact that it was halfway through the morning and he had things he needed to do.

Downstairs in the kitchen Georgia was nursing a mug of hot coffee whilst telling Ben severely, 'You shouldn't have taken his shoe, Ben.'

Soulfully he looked back at her. Previously, whilst she had known that Piers did not approve of Ben as a pet for his godmother, she had assumed that that was his main objection to the dog, but now...

Her heart missed a small beat as she remembered the look of bitter resentment Piers had given poor Ben. A look almost of hatred, and... And what? Georgia closed

her eyes, not wanting to give a name to the look she
thought she had seen in Piers's eyes, and then opened
them again as she heard Piers opening the kitchen door.
He was dressed in a snug-fitting pair of faded jeans and
a soft cotton shirt, and his shoes... She exhaled her
breath in a sigh as she saw the casual footwear he had
on.

As he followed the direction of her gaze Piers gave
Ben a hard look.

'It wasn't his fault.' Georgia quickly defended the
dog, seeing it. 'I...I should have kept an eye on him.'

She tensed as she saw the way Piers's mouth was
curling with contempt and derision, but he made no
comment, simply sitting down and starting to look
through the letters he had in his hand.

One of them was from the estate agent, and Piers
frowned as he read it. The agents were pressing him to
make a decision on the farmhouse he had viewed, reminding him that another would-be purchaser had expressed an interest in it.

Piers discovered that he had suddenly lost interest in
acquiring any kind of large potential family house...
What need did he have for one after all? A modern
apartment would surely be far more convenient, and, if
necessary, he could rent separate office accommodation.

He was glad that he had come to his senses before
he had done anything so foolish as being tempted to put
in an offer for the farmhouse, he told himself grimly.

After a couple of hours during which Piers and Georgia
occupied themselves in different parts of the house—
Piers doing some work whilst Georgia had an intensive
training session with Ben—they accidentally found

themselves in the kitchen together, having lunch. Little was said as they ate their respective meals.

As the silence between them stretched into a tautness that made Georgia's nerve-endings tingle with apprehension, she wondered unhappily how much of Piers's obvious antipathy towards her was actually caused by Ben's crime of destroying his shoe and how much by Piers's own regret about what he had said to her the previous evening. Well, if he thought she was silly enough to have taken any of what he had implied seriously...

Her head lifted proudly and, standing up, she called quietly to Ben, 'Come on, boy, time for our walk.'

'No...' Piers's sharp denial cut through the hostile atmosphere of the kitchen like a gunshot.

'No,' he repeated, ignoring the way Georgia's hand crept protectively towards the dog's collar. '*I'll* take him. Let's just see how much improvement you have been able to make with this so-called training you've been giving him. Not very much at all, if the events of the last few days are anything to go by,' he added sardonically.

Georgia's heart started to beat uncomfortably fast.

It was true that Ben was responding to what she was teaching him, but it was also true that he was a very independently minded dog, a free spirit of the canine world, so to speak, who, regrettably, had been used to being the pack leader for so long that he was reluctant to give up his role without something of a tussle.

Human beings, as he had made more than plain to Georgia over the last few days, were there to feed him and be protected by him; he had a very male and macho attitude towards *that* part of his canine heritage, as Georgia had noticed on their walks; for whenever a strange man happened to walk past them Ben immediately became very much the protective male dog guarding one of his pack. But it had to be admitted that human beings were not, in Ben's considered opinion, his superiors in the pack pecking order, an assumption which Georgia had been doing her best to alter skilfully. However, she was becoming increasingly aware that Ben needed rather more than mere training. What Ben actually needed was a visit to a pet psychologist. However, she could well imagine Piers's reaction were she to put this suggestion to him.

'I...I don't think he's quite ready for that yet,' she said instead, only to have Piers openly jeer at her as he asked her silkily,

'What exactly are you trying to say? That I was right all along and that the dog is untrainable?'

'*No* dog is untrainable,' Georgia defended swiftly. 'And Ben is a very intelligent animal.'

'An intelligent animal who needs a new home,' Piers agreed.

Fear and anger flashed through Georgia's eyes.

'You're determined to get rid of him, aren't you? You won't even give him a fair chance. Have you any idea what it could do to him emotionally to be re-homed? Have you *no* feelings, *no* compassion...*no* perception? Have you no—?'

'I've got a pair of ruined handmade shoes and a list of complaints that—' Piers began sardonically, but Georgia cut through them all, her protective female urges coming to the fore as she sensed Ben's growing danger.

'Is that *all* that matters to you?' she demanded heatedly. 'Material possessions, other people's opinions? Your godmother *loves* Ben; she—'

'She only took him on because of you,' Piers interrupted her furiously, 'so don't talk to *me* about feelings, because that was a piece of deliberate and cold-blooded manipulation and—'

'It was no such thing. I had nothing to do with your godmother's decision to give Ben a home,' Georgia denied defensively.

'You mean you aren't going to admit to having anything to do with it,' Piers countered coldly, 'but you *do* have to admit that there is no way that that dog is a suitable pet for my godmother...'

'You really hate Ben, don't you?' Georgia accused him. 'If you want my opinion, you don't just not like him, you're jealous of him as well.'

No sooner were the words out of her mouth than Georgia wished passionately that she had not uttered them; but it was too late. Piers was looking at her with an expression that made her quake in her shoes.

'Don't be ridiculous,' Piers told her curtly, getting off his chair and walking determinedly towards Ben whilst Georgia looked on helplessly.

'I really don't think this is a good idea,' she said quickly.

'Why?' Piers challenged her. 'Or do I already know the answer? You're afraid that I'll discover that far from improving Ben's behaviour—'

'It *is* improving,' Georgia insisted fiercely. 'It's just that my training programme is at a very delicate stage,' she improvised, 'and I'm concerned that it will confuse Ben having two different people giving him commands.'

The thin smile Piers gave her warned Georgia how easily he had seen through her desperate subterfuge.

'Really? Then how on earth is my godmother going to control him if the only person he's going to respond to is you, and the only commands he's going to respond to are yours?'

'I didn't say that,' Georgia protested. 'It's just that, right now…'

'Why not let me be my own judge of just how much progress he's making?' Piers challenged her softly, then snapped his fingers and said firmly, 'Ben, here…'

To Georgia's relief Ben immediately got up and trotted over to Piers's side.

Perhaps she was worrying too much, she tried to comfort herself five minutes later as Piers and Ben left the house, Ben walking perfectly to heel on his lead. Perhaps Ben might, with some canine perception, sense that he was being judged, and why, and might behave as she had been training him to do. Crossing her fingers, Georgia prayed inwardly that he would.

Thank goodness she had been sensible enough to realise in time just what a fatal mistake it would be for her to allow herself to fall in love with Piers. Just imagine the heartache she would have to suffer if she did so. It was obvious what a low opinion he had of her, even if physically he had…

But no, she wasn't going to allow herself to think about that, she told herself firmly. No, not for one minute…one *second*… Just because when Piers had touched her, when he'd kissed her, she had felt…wanted…had dreamed…

Two miles down the river footpath Piers had to concede that Ben was behaving with perfect canine manners, not pulling on his lead, walking quietly to heel, sitting on command and even sharing a disapproving look with Piers when another less well behaved canine chased after a passing cat.

'Very clever,' Piers told the dog dryly, 'but that doesn't alter the fact that you dug up the colonel's prize plants or the fact that you chewed my shoe.'

Happily Ben wagged his tail.

Nor did it alter the fact that, so far as Georgia was concerned, there was no contest about who came first in her affections, and it certainly wasn't him, Piers acknowledged grimly. It had hurt him to be accused of hating Ben so unjustly; he didn't hate the dog at all; he simply felt that he wasn't a suitable pet for his godmother.

'You're a man's dog,' he told Ben severely. 'You need to know who's boss.' He would be a wonderful family pet, though, Piers acknowledged as Ben paused to let a woman walking in the opposite direction with two young children admire and stroke him.

As Piers put Ben through his paces he was forced to concede that Georgia was doing an excellent job. Ben behaved perfectly, responding immediately to every command but, at the same time, exhibiting a kind of dignity that made it plain that his obedience came on his own terms and because it was what *he* wanted to do. As he praised him for his good behaviour and Ben wagged his tail, enjoying the fuss being made of him, Piers acknowledged that, under different circumstances, he could have become very fond of the dog.

'Come on, boy,' he instructed. 'Time to go home.'

Home! Ben's ears pricked up. Home meant food and Georgia.

They were almost back when Piers suddenly remembered that he needed to get in touch with the estate agent. It would be as easy to get in his car and drive into town and see the man as telephone him, he decided, and that way he could tell him that he had changed his mind about both properties and intended to look for something smaller.

He had his car keys with him, but he also had Ben. Frowning a little, he looked from the dog to the car and then, shrugging his shoulders, unlocked the car door and opened the rear door for the dog.

Immediately Ben hopped in and settled himself on the rear seat happily—Piers already knew that he was quite comfortable about travelling in the car. Closing the door, he got into the driver's seat and then activated the electric windows to make sure that the dog had enough fresh air. It was a warm day, not too hot for a human being, but Ben was a dog with a thick coat and Piers was mindful of the fact that he needed a cooler environment.

The car park opposite the town square on to which the estate agent's office fronted had a couple of empty parking spaces, but neither of them offered the kind of shade he felt that Ben needed so, instead, he turned down a small side street, parking his car on the shady side of the road and leaving the rear windows and the sun roof open enough to allow Ben plenty of fresh air.

He wouldn't be gone long.

'Good boy,' he told Ben as he walked away. Ben thumped his tail and settled happily on the seat. He liked travelling in cars, and it was very pleasant lying here in the shade where he could watch the world go by.

There were several cars parked on the narrow side street, but only one of them interested the two youths who slid deftly in and out of the shadows, trying every car door they passed, more out of habit than any real interest as they headed for Piers's car. They had been watching as Piers parked the large, gleaming Jaguar, their boredom momentarily lifting as they studied the car's sleek lines.

'No good for ram-raiding,' one of them said to the other, shaking his head.

'Nah,' the other agreed. 'Cool for speed, though. We could really give the cops a run for their money in that.'

Now, whilst one of them watched the street, the other quickly forced the lock on the driver's door. He knew exactly how to do so, and how to deactivate the car's alarm system and start the engine. After all, he had had plenty of practice, most of it whilst he was still under the legal age to drive.

As the two youths slid into the car, Ben gave a low growl, but as they turned up the sound of the radio and searched for a preferred station neither of them heard it.

On the pedestrian crossing a young mother with a small child and an elderly man both shot indignant, frightened looks after the departing speeding car, making its two occupants laugh, but to their disappointment, as they raced past the town's police station, there was no one there to witness their provocative behaviour, no striped police car to pursue them and give chase, adding to the excitement and exhilaration of their afternoon.

They knew the town and its environs even better than any cop could possibly do, they were fond of boasting, and they had safe places where they could hide out, garages they could drive into whilst the police searched for them.

This car, like all the others they had stolen, would end up either wrecked or broken up for 'spares'.

As they shot across a roundabout, causing other drivers to brake and swerve, they both laughed, whilst in the back Ben growled.

*　　*　　*

Piers was longer in the estate agent's than he had expected, his original decision to tell the agent that he had decided against both the properties he had viewed oddly overturned by the sight of a photograph in the window of the farmhouse. Looking at it, Piers had undergone an unfamiliar wavering and a totally unexpected and unwanted change of heart.

'The farmhouse?' the agent queried, frowning. 'But I thought…'

'I'm prepared to offer them the full asking price,' Piers heard himself telling the agent, 'on the condition that they move out almost immediately.'

The agent's frown deepened.

'But I thought you said that you wanted…' His voice tailed off as he saw the look in Piers's eyes. 'I'll telephone the vendors now and put your offer to them,' he offered instead.

Ten minutes later, as he walked out of the estate agent's office, Piers had committed himself to buying the farmhouse. Was he totally and completely mad?

He started to walk a little faster, unwilling to pursue his own thoughts, and then came to an abrupt halt as he turned into the street where he had left his car and saw someone else had parked where he had expected to find his Jaguar—and Ben! A quick check of the street confirmed that there were no signs anywhere warning against parking and threatening clamping and removal of vehicles should anyone do so, convincing Piers that his car had not been removed by some righteous corporation official.

Out of the corner of his eye he saw a police patrol car turning into the street and immediately he hailed the driver, quickly explaining to him that his car appeared to have gone missing.

'And the registration number of the vehicle, sir?' the police officer asked him politely.

Tersely Piers gave it to him.

'There was a dog in the car,' Piers told the officer, 'and to be honest I'm more concerned about him than I am about the vehicle.'

As he spoke Piers realised, a little to his own astonishment, that it was the truth. His first thought when he had realised that his car had gone had been for Ben.

'A dog, you say?' The policeman frowned.

Ten minutes later Piers was at the police station reporting the theft of his car—and Ben—in more detail.

'Look,' he told the police officer taking his statement. 'If it will help I'm fully prepared to offer a financial reward...'

The police officer pursed his lips.

'I doubt it will do any good, sir,' he told Piers politely. 'It's more than likely that the car—'

'It's not the return of the car that concerns me,' Piers interrupted him. 'The reward would be for the safe return of Ben, the dog...'

'We'll do our best, sir,' was the police officer's courteous response as Piers signed his statement and got up to leave.

Georgia looked anxiously at the kitchen clock. She had been expecting Piers back with Ben ages ago. Where was he? Where were they? Had Ben misbehaved, perhaps even run off, refusing to come back? She closed her eyes. She could just imagine how Piers would react to *that*. 'Oh, Ben,' she pleaded under her breath, 'please, please be good.' In championing the dog she knew that she had destroyed whatever slim chance there might have been of Piers changing his opinion about her, and...

And what? Falling in love with her, feeling something much, much more than mere unemotional sexual desire for her? How *could* she have deserted Ben, though? How could she possibly have wanted a love that came with that kind of price tag? And besides, she didn't want Piers's love, did she?

She started up as she heard the front door being opened. The *front* door. A small feather of alarm curled through her stomach. Piers would never bring Ben in through the front door after a long walk, risking the dog's muddy paws on his godmother's elegant carpets.

When Piers opened the kitchen door Georgia was standing with her back to the kitchen table, the same table on which he had threatened so sensuously, so *temptingly*, to make love to her. Her body tensed.

'Where's Ben?' she demanded as soon as Piers walked in.

As he heard the accusatory note in her voice and saw the look in her eyes, Piers felt his heart sink.

It was going to be so hard to tell her what had happened... The fear he could see in her eyes only mirrored his own feelings of concern for the dog. He was a man who was used to being in control of things, and to have to acknowledge not just to himself but to Georgia as well that he had no control over what was happening, no way of guaranteeing Ben's safety, of promising her that all would be well, was dealing a very hard blow to his in-built male sense of self. And because of that he responded in a way which he later was forced to admit was a world away from the gentle care with which he had been planning to break the news to her all the way back to the house.

'Is that all you can think about?' he demanded shortly instead. 'The dog? Well...'

As she heard the anger in his voice and her senses picked up the guilt that underlined it Georgia immediately accused him, 'Something's happened to him, hasn't it? You've done something to him. If he's been hurt... If you've hurt him...'

If *he'd* hurt him? Piers opened his mouth to defend himself and then closed it again. What, after all, could he say? He *was* responsible for Ben being put in a position where he could be hurt, even if he had done so by accident rather than by design.

Too anxious about Ben's absence to interpret correctly the look in Piers's eyes, Georgia only knew that his silence totally condemned him.

'Where is he? What have you done with him?' she demanded, her voice breaking on a small sob of anguished despair as she mentally visualised poor Ben locked up in a cage, waiting to be found a new owner, not understanding what had happened to him.

There was no way she was going to allow Ben to be hurt like that. If she spoke to her parents, explained the situation, she knew full well that they would generously help her to fund the purchase of her own small property, somewhere where *she* could have a dog. Yes, if necessary *she* would give Ben a home herself rather than...

'Where is he?' she repeated fiercely. *'Where?'*

'I don't know,' Piers told her gruffly. The sight of the tears she was trying valiantly to hide had brought a lump of emotion to his own throat.

'You're lying,' Georgia accused him wildly. 'You've taken him somewhere—a kennels or somewhere—and you've *left* him there...just because he's...he's a bit...independent and— Have you any idea what it does to an animal to be abandoned like that?' she asked him in a choked voice. 'Have you any idea of how your godmother will feel? Have you given any thought to the feelings of—? But you *don't* care, do you? You don't care about anyone else's feelings. All *you* care about is your precious shoes,' she denounced him scathingly.

'For heaven's sake, will you just listen?' Piers said sharply. 'I have *not* taken Ben to a kennels. Nor have I abandoned him. I...'

'Then where is he?' Georgia demanded, her face flushing with emotion and her eyes brilliant with a mixture of tears and passion as she deliberately held his gaze, daring him to lie to her.

'I...I wish to God I knew,' Piers groaned, with such feeling that Georgia shivered, a cold finger of dread icing down her spine.

'What...what happened?' she asked him shakily. 'If he slipped his lead and ran off, refusing to come back, it's just a game he likes to play. If you'd waited... Tell me where it happened; I'll go out and look for him...'

'No, it...isn't as simple as that,' Piers told her, catching hold of her arm as she made to hurry past him to the back door, her mind already mentally visualising the familiar river walk she took Ben on every day and the potential spots where he liked to break free of her to investigate rabbit scents.

'Ben was in my car,' Piers told her heavily, 'and the car has been stolen.'

'What?' Georgia stared at him. 'I don't believe you,' she told him furiously, her face burning with a mixture of anger and scorn. Did he really think she was so stupid as to fall for something like that?

'You were taking Ben for a *walk*. You never said

anything about driving him anywhere in your car,' she added suspiciously. 'You…'

'I decided to call round and see the estate agent,' Piers told her wearily.

'No! I don't believe you,' Georgia repeated stubbornly. 'You're lying.'

Her heart, she had discovered, was beginning to beat frighteningly fast as she tried to grapple with the implications of what Piers was telling her. It wasn't true, of course; he was simply lying to her to cover himself for what he had really done. After all, he had threatened often enough to have Ben re-homed, but now that he had taken active steps to do so he was refusing to admit it, covering his cruel behaviour with a cowardly lie.

Her face burning with anger and indignation, she told him fiercely, shakily, 'I think you've now insulted me in just about every way there is. Professionally and… and sexually…and now mentally by…by making up a story that no one could possibly believe. You've been determined to get rid of Ben right from the start. I realise now that it wouldn't have made any difference how obedient I'd taught him to be, would it?' she said, biting down hard on her bottom lip to control the tears threatening to fill her eyes.

She continued painfully, 'You *wanted* me to fail. You wanted Ben to fail so that you could have an excuse for getting rid of him. In fact it wouldn't surprise me now to discover that you deliberately encouraged him to chew your shoes—your *handmade* leather shoes,' she emphasised angrily. 'But you're simply not man enough to tell your godmother outright that you intended to get rid of her dog, are you? So you had to do it in an underhanded way, using poor Ben's naughtiness…blaming him…blaming me…'

Georgia could feel her mouth trembling wildly as her emotions threatened to betray her completely. It wasn't just Ben she was defending…fighting for…it was herself too. Her own integrity, her own emotions…her own love… *Love!*

Shock stabbed through her, stopping her breath, her face going white with the pain of it as right at the heart of her anger she discovered the reason why Piers's duplicity and cowardliness hurt so much.

She *couldn't* love him. It just wasn't possible. She hated him, despised him. She…

Now she was crying—dry, desperate tears that shook her body and tore at Piers's heart.

Despite everything she had said, all the accusations she had thrown at him, all the passionate loyalty she had shown to Ben—or perhaps *because* of it—he couldn't sustain the righteous anger he knew he should feel. All he wanted to do, all he ached to do, was to take her in his arms and comfort her, to reassure her that he would search the length and breadth of the country—of the *world* if need be—to find Ben and prove to her just how wrong she was.

Impulsively Piers took a step towards her, stopping dead, a muscle twitching in his jaw, as he saw the way Georgia was looking at him, her expression, her whole body tight and frozen with rejection.

Georgia shivered. Just for a moment she had thought that Piers was going to reach out and touch her… comfort her… That just showed the state she was in— the vulnerability of her emotions. But what was even worse was that for a small space of time she had actually felt impelled to go towards him, to betray by her body language just how much she longed for and needed the comfort of his arms around her, the reassurance of his voice telling her that everything was going to be all right, that Ben was safe, that she had misunderstood.

Both of them tensed as they heard someone ringing the front doorbell.

Predictably, or so it seemed to Georgia, Piers got to the front door before she did, opening it and then demanding quickly as he gestured to the police officer standing outside to come in, 'Have you found him? Is he...?'

The officer, briefed by his colleagues, had heard how the owner of the expensive car which had been stolen from the town was far more concerned about the fate of the dog which had been in the car than the vehicle itself. He sympathised. He had a dog himself, and two children who would be distraught if anything similar should happen to it.

'No, I'm afraid we haven't, sir; however, there is some news on the car. Apparently a lorry driver reported seeing a car that matches the description of yours being driven erratically on the motorway going north. We've alerted all the motorway units, but so far none of them have seen anything.

'You mentioned in your statement that the car had an almost full tank of petrol,' he added with a faint sigh that fell just short of being gently reproving.

'Unfortunately, yes,' Piers agreed, whilst Georgia, who had overheard everything the police officer had said, stood rigidly in the hallway, her face white and her heart thumping.

Piers hadn't lied to her after all. He had told her the truth. His car had been stolen with Ben in it. She swallowed hard. She obviously owed him an apology.

'We think we've got a pretty good idea of the identity

of the pair who've taken the car,' the police officer was continuing. 'The lorry driver reported two occupants, both of them young males, and we established that two local youths who have a record for taking cars without the owners' permission and using them for joyriding are missing from their usual haunts in the town. It's a pity the car had a full tank of petrol; however, on the plus side, the fact that they've driven it on to the motorway suggests that they will simply use it for joyriding and then, once the tank is empty, dump it somewhere.'

'Never mind about the car,' Piers told him. 'What about Ben, the dog? Did the lorry driver...?'

The policeman shook his head.

'No. There was no report about any dog, but...' He paused and looked uncertainly at Georgia, whose pale, set face gave away her anxiety. 'The fact that there hasn't been any sighting suggests...er...that the dog must still be in the car...'

He meant that the youths hadn't opened the door and pushed Ben out onto the motorway, Georgia guessed, correctly interpreting his coded words. She was a vet, after all, and she had had experience of dogs being thus treated, sometimes by their owners, but that didn't stop her eyes filling with panicky tears or her hand going up to her mouth to stifle the small sound of pain she could feel rising in her throat.

'He's a large, heavy dog,' Piers said quickly. 'I doubt he could be easily ejected from the car if he didn't want to be.'

'Try not to worry,' the police officer told Georgia gruffly. 'Sometimes these joyriders have radios that allow them to listen in to police frequencies, so we're broadcasting a message that there'll be a substantial re-

ward for the return of the dog—just as you asked us to,'
he told Piers.

Piers had offered a *reward* for Ben's safe return.
Georgia could feel her face going scarlet with mortification.

'You'll let us know just as soon as you hear anything?' Piers was requesting the police officer as he
turned to leave.

Confirming that he would, he stepped out of the front
door, leaving Piers to close it behind him.

As they stood together in the hallway Georgia took a
deep breath and closed her eyes, opening them almost
immediately as she tried to draw on her rapidly deplet-
ing store of inner strength.

'I'm very sorry about what I said about you...about
you hurting Ben and lying about what had happened to
him,' she said, starting her apologies with the words
carefully spaced apart, but then rushing over them so
that one virtually ran into the other as she finished
quickly, 'I owe you an apology and I...I shouldn't have
said what I did,' she concluded huskily.

I only said it because it hurt so much that I loved you
and that you didn't love me back and that you couldn't
be the man I wanted you to be, Georgia could have
further explained to him, but what was the point when
to do so would only expose her to further pain? What
mattered most right now was not her own feelings, her
own anguished awareness of how much she loved Piers
and how impossible it was that her love could ever be
returned, but Ben.

'No doubt you had your reasons for thinking as you
did,' Piers told her curtly. It still hurt that she could
have thought him capable of something so cruel and
cowardly. His pride still smarted from the blows she had

dealt it, but what hurt him far more was knowing how low an opinion she had of him. He *had* been jealous of Ben, yes—jealous of the way she had taken the dog's side against him, so to speak, when Ben had chewed his shoe. And, yes, perhaps it had been wrong of him to resent the love she seemed to lavish so tenderly on the dog, whilst treating him with such contempt and scorn, but...

'I really am sorry,' Georgia repeated dully, unable to bring herself to look into his eyes, already knowing the indifference she would no doubt see there. Why should Piers care how dreadful she felt? Her feelings were of no concern to him whatsoever!

CHAPTER SEVEN

CAUTIOUSLY Ben poked his nose up towards the half-open rear window of the car, carefully sniffing the air. Country air, he could tell, but not the type of country air that was familiar to him. This air had a different scent about it.

He had been deliberately keeping a low profile under the rug in the rear of the car where he had been asleep when the car had been stolen, controlling his initial reaction to bark warningly at the strangers who had driven off in Piers's car—the car it was his duty to protect! Intuition had quickly told him that the two men were dangerous and should be left alone. Ben was no coward, but...!

Even more cautiously he looked towards the front of the car, where the two strangers who had driven him off were lolling, half asleep, in a drunken stupor. They had stopped several miles away, having chased a small sports car driven by a pretty girl off the motorway and down a series of narrow, twisting country lanes, hurling taunting comments to her as they did so. She had finally escaped them by driving in through some electronic gates to a large house where the two youths had appeared to decide not to follow.

They had then driven on until they had reached a small village, where they had driven on to the pavement outside a small store, leaving the car engine running whilst they went inside and threatened the shopkeeper, laughing at his distress whilst they took what they wanted from his shelves.

Drinking and swearing at any other unfortunate motorists they'd chanced to come across—fortunately only a few in this remote country area of the Yorkshire Dales—they had finally brought the car to a halt.

'Better stop,' one had told the other. 'Not much petrol left. Need to find a garage…'

'Won't find one up here…' the other had replied, before emptying the can he had been drinking from and throwing it out of the car window.

It was a warm night and they had opened all the electric windows. In the front seat the one doing the driving woke up now and said to the other, 'Come on, we need petrol.' He was just starting up the car engine when Ben saw his chance and seized it, jumping quickly through the open window.

'What's that?' the other youth demanded, suddenly alert as he swivelled round in his seat, staring at where Ben was streaking away into the dusk-shrouded countryside.

'Dunno; I didn't see anything.'

'It was a dog…there was a dog here in the car…'

'No way,' the driver scoffed. 'You've had too much to drink…and I haven't had enough. Come on, let's go and find some more booze…'

'And some girls…' his companion suggested.

Booze, girls and petrol… 'Yeah, cool,' the driver agreed.

Ben watched from a safe distance as they turned the car round and drove off. The evening air was different from the air at home. There was no river smell for one thing. But he could smell *something*… On the hillside he heard the baaing of sheep followed by the cry of a fox. Foxes Ben knew...sheep he did not!

Georgia woke up abruptly. It had been gone midnight before she and Piers had acknowledged that there was no useful purpose to be served in either of them staying up any longer. Neither of them had been able to eat the supper which Piers had insisted on preparing—heaping coals of fire indeed on her guilty head, Georgia had acknowledged later in bed. Anxiety for Ben had given Piers's face a rather distant and stern expression which had prevented her from trying to make conversation with him. Besides, what was the point? She had already said enough, hadn't she? *More* than enough!

Wide awake now, she flung back the bedclothes and, reaching for her cotton robe, pulled it on. Her throat ached with suppressed tears and her mouth felt dry. Perhaps if she went downstairs and made herself a cup of tea it might help to soothe her back to sleep.

Where was Ben now? Was he still in the car or...? As she reached the kitchen she came to an abrupt halt. Piers was already there, standing in front of the window, watching the slow fingers of the false dawn stroking across the sky.

As she switched on the light he turned round, his mouth hardening when he saw her. Quite plainly her company wasn't welcome to him, Georgia acknowledged, and she tried not to betray the fact that her senses were telling her that beneath the robe he had pulled on he was probably completely naked.

What on earth was she doing, thinking about something like that at such a time? The inappropriateness of her thoughts coupled with their sensuality made her face burn with shamed self-consciousness.

There was poor Ben, dognapped and in heaven alone knew what kind of danger and fear, and here she was thinking…longing…fantasising…

'I just came down for a cup of tea,' she told Piers jerkily. 'I couldn't sleep.' Involuntarily both of them looked towards Ben's empty bed.

Piers could feel a raw, tight feeling at the back of his throat. This afternoon when he had been walking Ben they had chanced to cross the path of a very attractive brunette walking her dog. Ben had turned to Piers, and Piers could have sworn the look the dog gave him was totally that of one heterosexual male to another. Stupid, of course. A dog was just a dog, and there was no way he, Piers, had ever allowed himself to be sentimental about animals and certainly no way he had ever fallen into the trap of imbuing them with human characteristics.

Georgia could feel her eyes filling with tears.

'Do you think the police *will* find him?' she asked Piers eagerly, unable to keep the longing for reassurance out of her voice.

Piers swallowed and responded far too heartily.

'Oh, yes, I'm sure they will. Sooner or later whoever has taken the car is either going to abandon it or drive into a garage to fill it with petrol, and when they do…'

Almost as though on cue the telephone suddenly rang, but for a moment neither of them made to answer it.

Piers didn't believe a word of what he had just told her; Georgia could see it in his eyes. He was afraid of answering the phone, of hearing what might be said, as she was herself, but just as she thought he was going to let it ring without answering it Piers strode across the room and picked up the receiver.

'Yes. I see,' Georgia heard him saying grimly. 'Well,

yes, I'm sure it is, but right now I'm not so concerned about that. What about...?'

'No...he wasn't there; the garage owner didn't see any sign of him,' the police officer on the other end of the line told Piers.

'Have you questioned the lads?'

'No. Both of them are too drunk to question, but they're in custody and once they've sobered up...'

As Piers hung up and turned to Georgia she guessed what he was going to say.

'They've found the car,' he told her gruffly. 'They tried to fill it with petrol and then drive off without paying, but the garage owner called the police, who managed to catch up with them.'

'Ben?' Georgia asked anxiously, but she already knew the answer before she saw Piers shaking his head.

'No sign of him,' he told her heavily, avoiding looking at her as he advised her, 'The police aren't going to question the two youths who took the car until they've sobered up, so why don't you go back to bed for what's left of the night and try to get some sleep? You won't be doing yourself any good, nor Ben either, by staying down here worrying,' he pointed out gently.

And no doubt he didn't want to have to cope with her misery or endure her company, Georgia guessed as she dutifully headed towards the stairs.

Five minutes later, though, back in her bed, she knew that sleep was going to be impossible. Ben... Where *was* he? What had happened to him? Just the thought of him being exposed to the busy traffic of a motorway made her heart stand still. She had taught him to sit and wait before they crossed any road, but... But a motorway wasn't a road...

Only by gripping her bottom lip between her teeth

was Georgia able to hold back the small cry of anguish bubbling in her throat, and she was still biting into it, trying to suppress her fear, when Piers rapped briefly on her bedroom door seconds later and then came in carrying a cup of tea.

'Somehow I didn't think you'd be asleep,' he told her wryly as he indicated the tea he was carrying and told her, 'Tea, the universal British panacea—so they say...'

Georgia released her bottom lip and tried to smile.

'It's kind of you to take the trouble—' she began stiltedly, and then had to stop as a betraying sob choked off her voice and shook her body.

'Oh, Georgia,' she heard Piers groaning, and then he was sitting on the bed next to her, wrapping her comfortingly in his arms.

'I keep thinking about poor Ben trying to cross the motorway,' Georgia sobbed. 'He doesn't...he won't...'

'Don't,' Piers groaned. 'If only I hadn't put him in the car.'

'You weren't to know that it was going to be stolen,' Georgia tried to protest, and then, as she saw the look of desolation in his eyes, her heart was rocked with tender compassion for him and she told him softly, 'You mustn't blame yourself; it isn't your fault...'

'Yes, it is,' Piers insisted, 'but I promise you, Georgia, I never meant him any harm. I was jealous of him when you insisted on defending him...protecting him from my anger,' he admitted gruffly, drawing Georgia's head down against his shoulder and leaning his chin on it so that she couldn't see in his eyes the real reason for his jealousy, and so that he couldn't see in hers her compassion and the knowledge that she didn't return his love.

'It seemed as though everything he did was right and

everything I did was wrong. I could see in your eyes how much you despised me for complaining because he had chewed my shoe...'

'No!' Georgia protested quickly, lifting her head to look into his eyes before he could stop her. 'I never despised you; I was just afraid...afraid that you might insist on sending Ben away.' She bit her lip again. 'You see, I knew...know, really...that you were—*are* right when you say that he isn't really a suitable pet for your godmother. What he really needs is—'

She stopped as Piers supplied for her, 'A family.'

Georgia swallowed hard as she nodded.

'But your godmother loves him, and he's already been rejected once.'

'And your tender heart can't bear to think of him being hurt again.'

'I hate hurting anything...or...or anyone,' Georgia admitted in a low voice.

'Right now, I'm badly in need of some of that TLC of yours,' Piers told her huskily, bending his head closer to hers.

Georgia took a deep breath and tried to keep still. If she so much as moved an inch...a *centimetre*...her lips would almost be touching Piers's. Had what he had just said to her been the invitation it seemed, or did he just mean that he wanted her understanding? The cotton nightdress she was wearing was only thin with tiny shoestring straps but she felt unbearably hot in it, as though her whole body was on fire. Whatever she did, though, she must not give in to the temptation to look at Piers's mouth, because if she did...

'Nothing to say?' Piers whispered, his words so faint that she had to lean closer just to catch them.

But leaning closer was a fatal mistake, and her glance

was drawn helplessly from the deep open V of Piers's robe all the way up the bronzed expanse of his naked chest, with its soft sprinkling of richly silky body hair, up past his Adam's apple, so tautly masculine in a throat that just begged to be touched and kissed, right to his mouth.

His mouth!

Georgia swallowed helplessly, totally unable to drag her transfixed gaze away from the tormenting temptation it was feasting on. Just looking at Piers's mouth made her want to reach out and touch it, to trace its shape with her fingertip, memorising its shape and texture so that she could then re-draw it, sketching its every angle with soft butterfly kisses, before...

As though he was reading her thoughts as they formed, she heard Piers telling her urgently, 'Do it, Georgia. Oh, God, yes...' he breathed thickly as her wide-eyed, bemused gaze met the sensual intimacy of his. 'Yes,' he repeated rawly. 'Kiss me...'

But as his mouth fastened over hers he was the one doing the kissing, his lips hungrily devouring hers, his arms tightening around her as he drew her closer.

Delicious tremors of excitement shivered down Georgia's spine as her mouth, her *body* responded helplessly to him.

'Piers... Piers...' She could hear herself moaning his name against his mouth as she clung to him, her hands gripping the edges of his robe and then releasing it as her fingertips accidentally brushed against his hot skin and fiery darts of pleasure acted like magnets, fusing her fingertips and then the whole of her hands to his body as she slid them beneath his robe, exploring the hard breadth of his chest. Her whole body was burning with arousal and longing now, aching to be touched...caressed...possessed...

'Piers!' As she gasped his name, helpless to defend herself from what she was feeling, he seemed to sense her confusion, gentling his kiss.

He told her fiercely, 'It's all right...it's all right. I feel the same way. I want you so much it hurts,' he added, groaning out loud as he ran his hand down her nightdress-clad back and closed his eyes.

'Let me take this off, Georgia,' he begged her. 'Let me see you...all of you...'

Just for a moment Georgia hesitated. She was by nature very modest—too much so, she sometimes thought—but as though he guessed what she was thinking Piers whispered to her gently, 'You want to see me too, don't you? You want to touch me...hold me...'

Her breath catching in her throat, Georgia gave a soft, panting gasp of assent. What he was suggesting, offering, was too alluring, too tempting for her to refuse, her eyes already glistening with emotion at the thought of the sensual riches he was promising her.

'Let me take this off, then,' he told her, carefully sliding the straps of her nightdress free of her shoulders. Even that light touch of his fingertips against her naked skin was enough to bring her out in a mass of sensually aroused goosebumps, and Georgia knew before her nightdress slid free of her naked body, to reveal them in all their darkly pink, feminine glory, that her nipples were as eagerly aroused as two rosebuds, just waiting for the hot, silky warmth of the morning sun to coax them into full flower.

Only what her nipples yearned for was not the touch of the summer sun, but the stroke of Piers's fingers; the moist heat of his mouth. The intimacy of her own thoughts was enough to make her shudder visibly.

He had never seen a woman betray her arousal, her need, so innocently nor so proudly, Piers acknowledged, and he had certainly never felt so awed, so humbled, so *blessed* in knowing *he* was the reason for that arousal.

She might not love him but Georgia wanted him, and somehow he knew instinctively that this level of desire was as unfamiliar to her as loving her so intensely was unfamiliar to him.

Very carefully he reached out and cupped her naked breasts, looking first into her eyes and then down to the silken globes he was cherishing with his hands and his gaze, before telling her thickly, 'You are so beautiful...so perfect...'

'No...' Georgia began to deny, but before she could finish he was kissing her, gently at first, and then with increasing passion as he slid his hands around her back, bringing her naked breasts into direct contact with the warm, silky abrasion of his chest. Georgia thought the sensation of his body pressed so close to hers, his heart pumping so strongly that it could have been beating for both of them, was going to make her faint.

'No one else has ever done this with you before, have they?' Piers asked her insistently, his emotions overruling his natural caution as the instinctive knowledge that she was giving herself to him with an intimacy she had never shared with anyone else hit him like a jolt of adrenaline released into his bloodstream.

As he spoke Piers's hand was returning to cover her naked breast with an open possessiveness that made Georgia's heart turn over inside her chest. Just for a moment, with that look in his eyes, she could *almost* convince herself that he loved her.

'If just my caressing your breast makes you feel like this,' Piers breathed hotly as he felt the mute shudders of delight run through her body, betraying everything that she was feeling to him, 'just think how it's going to feel when we do something more intimate.'

Something more intimate! Georgia's eyes started to widen with a mixture of excitement and alarm. She was already quivering so intensely with the extent of the arousal and longing coursing through her that she didn't think she could actually bear to endure any more pleasure. But Piers was already bending his head, whispering such things against her mouth and into her ears that her whole body burned to hear them—and burned even hotter to know them.

And then, somewhere in the town, a dog barked.

Immediately Georgia froze. Ben... Ben was stolen, lost, in danger, and here she was lying in Piers's arms, indulging herself selfishly, not even thinking about him.

'No,' she told Piers sharply, pushing him away, her eyes widening with distress at her own selfishness.

'No?' Piers tensed. Another few seconds and he would have been unable to stop himself from telling her how much he loved her, unable to stop himself from showing her how much he loved her. He ought to be grateful that she *had* stopped him and brought him to his senses. He was glad. There was no point in him making the situation between them even worse by declaring a love for her that she quite plainly did not want.

'I'm sorry,' he apologised distantly, averting his eyes as she scrabbled to retrieve her nightdress. 'That was...'

'It's all right,' Georgia told him breathlessly, praying inwardly that she could stop him before he explained to her that he had momentarily been overwhelmed by his male sexual drive; that his reaction to her had simply been that of a normal healthy male to the presence of a semi-naked woman. 'I understand. We're both upset about Ben... I know you just intended to comfort me... I...'

As he viewed her downbent head Piers's mouth twisted wryly.

'It wasn't exactly *comfort* that was uppermost in my mind just now when I—' he began.

But Georgia interrupted him in a choked voice, begging him, 'Please don't say any more. I'm not... I don't...'

She didn't love him; that was what she was finding so hard to say, Piers guessed.

'I guess you're right,' he agreed heavily. 'We're both acting somewhat out of character.'

Well, that was true enough in his case. He had certainly never come anywhere near telling any other woman that he loved her, but then he had never loved any other woman, had never felt about anyone else the way he felt about Georgia. His feelings for her were out of character...or, at least, outside his experience.

Outside, dawn proper was now peaching the sky. If Ben had survived the night, once the police had been able to interview the youths who had taken his car, perhaps they might be able to narrow down an area where they could begin searching for him. *If* he had survived the night. If he hadn't... If he hadn't, Georgia would never forgive him, and neither would he ever forgive himself.

CHAPTER EIGHT

KEEPING his body low to the ground, Ben followed the sound of the bleating sheep. He could see them now—white dots breaking up the darkness of the night-cloaked hills. They were high-country sheep, still with not yet fully grown lambs, and with his sharp senses Ben could see and smell the vixen shadowing an isolated group of three ewes, all with lambs, on the outskirts of the flock, her cubs at her heels.

As he watched the vixen carefully marking out her prey Ben growled deep in his throat. He wasn't a country dog, but both Mrs Latham and Georgia had strong views about such things, and Ben, who loved a good brisk run after a rabbit, knew much better than to try and catch one.

Ben did his best to growl a warning to the ewe, but he was too far away to prevent the inevitable. Even so... Cautiously he made his way towards the flock, but when he got there it was too late. Where there had been triplets now there were only two small lambs, both of them being hurried anxiously away by the ewe. Cautiously Ben dipped his head fastidiously, sniffing the scent of fresh blood.

The farmer, alerted to the intrusion by the sound of the farm dogs barking, was already halfway up the hill, gun at the ready, when he saw Ben. Immediately he took aim...

'Lost another lamb last night,' Harry Bowles complained to his brother-in-law grumpily as his wife poured both her husband and her brother a cup of strong Yorkshire tea. Her brother was in the police force and often called round to have breakfast with them at the end of his shift if he was working in the area.

'Fox?' Brian Jessop asked him sympathetically as he took his tea from his sister.

Harry Bowles shook his head.

'No,' he told him shortly. 'Dog. Saw him as plain as day. Incomer's dog, by the looks of him. Some fancy breed that—'

'What exactly did he look like?' Brian Jessop asked him sharply, putting down his tea.

Briefly Harry described Ben.

'You didn't shoot him, did you?' Brian asked him. 'Only it sounds to me like he's this dog that's been reported as being stolen, and there's a reward being offered for his safe return.'

'Tried, but I missed him, Brian,' Harry told him grimly.

'Come on; let's go and see if he's still around,' Brian Jessop suggested. 'If he's still about perhaps we can coax him down to the farm and get a proper look at him.'

Ben saw the two men from the small safe place he had found for himself in the shelter of an outcrop of rock overgrown with ferns and other vegetation. Warily he watched them. He recognised the farmer and stiffened anxiously. They were calling his name but he didn't know them, and in the last twenty-four hours Ben had learned that not all human beings were like his owners. Cautiously he watched the two men, only relaxing when, nearly half an hour later, they turned their backs on him and started to walk back in the direction they had come.

'I'll put a report in, then, just in case the dog you saw was this missing English setter,' Brian told his brother-in-law. 'And remember if you see him again to try and coax him down here to the farm...'

'If I see him worrying my sheep again it won't be coaxing him anywhere that I'll be wanting to do,' Harry told him grimly. It was bad enough being a farmer without having city folks' dogs worrying his sheep.

It was much later on in the day when Ben, driven by tiredness and hunger, finally succumbed to the temptation the farm represented. From his vantage point on the hillside he could see down into the farmyard, where Mary Bowles was feeding her husband's working dog accompanied by the elderly 'no breed' dog, Jack, who was her own pet.

Ben's mouth watered as he watched them eating their food. He was hungry. Very hungry.

Stealthily he started to make his way down the hill.

The collie sensed his presence first, setting up a sharp volley of barks which Jack quickly joined in. Mary Bowles heard them from the kitchen and hurried out into the yard. Harry was in town on business, and she wasn't expecting any visitors, but the sight of the one she saw sliding round the corner of the field wall made her gasp and call softly, 'Ben... Ben... Here, good dog...'

A *woman's* voice... Ben liked women. Eagerly he hurried into the yard, allowing Mary to fuss him and gratefully accepting the food she brought him, but when she tried to grab his collar Ben sensed danger and immediately darted out of her reach, heading swiftly back up the hill.

* * *

'Are you sure it was him?' Brian Jessop questioned his sister when she rang him.

'It was definitely the dog you described to us this morning,' Mary Bowles confirmed.

'Right. I'll tell them at the station, then. Pity you couldn't catch him.'

It was Piers who took the call from the police whilst Georgia was outside in the garden hanging up the cover from Ben's bed, which she had washed more to give herself something to do than anything else.

'That was the police,' Piers told her as she came back into the kitchen just as he was replacing the receiver. 'They've had a report of a sighting of Ben...'

'Where?' Georgia demanded immediately.

'In the Yorkshire Dales. A farmer's wife saw him in the farmyard and fed him, apparently, and—'

'He's safe...' Georgia breathed in relief, tears filling her eyes. 'Oh, thank God.'

'Don't get your hopes up too high,' Piers told her gently. 'Ben—if it *was* Ben—ran off as soon as she'd fed him. It seems that the farmer had taken a shot at Ben earlier in the day. It's sheep country up there, and—'

'Where is this farm?' Georgia asked him urgently. 'I want to go up there. If Ben is there—'

'*If* he is there...' Piers agreed, and then stopped. He could tell from Georgia's expression that she intended to go and hunt for Ben and that there was nothing he could do to stop her.

'Look, I've got the farm's telephone number. Let me give them a ring to ask them if they'd mind if we drove up and looked for Ben.'

Briefly Georgia hesitated. Her immediate instinct was

to jump in her car and drive north just as fast as she could, but what Piers was suggesting made sense.

'Very well,' she agreed reluctantly.

It seemed to her that, by some unspoken mutual pact, both of them had decided to put their own feelings and the intense complex issues which made up their personal relationship to one side, to concentrate on Ben's plight. The intimate events of the night had not been referred to by either of them during the long hours of the day whilst they'd waited for news of Ben, and now, even though she was not going to allow herself to admit it, secretly Georgia knew that she was glad to have Piers with her to share the anxiety and the wait. Not that she would ever admit as much to him, nor was she going to admit how relieved she was to have a respite from the hostility between them.

Piers's manner towards her now was one of almost gentle concern, one of almost protective care, one of almost loving maleness.

Now, *that* she knew she *had* to be imagining, because Piers most certainly did not love her. But she loved him.

As she waited for Piers to ring the Bowleses Georgia tried not to let her emotions swamp her. She was still, she suspected, a little bit in shock. To have gone so swiftly from believing that Piers had deliberately abandoned Ben to finding out the truth had left her feeling not just wrong-footed and guilty, but emotionally far too vulnerable and susceptible. Last night in Piers's arms...

But she must not think about that, or about any of the other things...pleasures...hopes...she had felt in the dark intimacy of the night. No. What she must think about right now was Ben and his safety.

'That's very kind of you,' she heard Piers saying warmly into the telephone receiver. 'Yes, we'll be leaving almost straight away, so it shouldn't be too long before we're with you.

'That was Mary Bowles,' he told Georgia when he had concluded his call. 'She was the one who saw Ben and fed him. She's convinced that it *is* Ben. She says that we're more than welcome to drive up there and stay with them whilst we look for him.'

'Oh, Piers.' Sharply painful tears filled Georgia's eyes and instinctively she started to move closer to him.

Just as instinctively Piers recognised her need, closing the gap between them and opening his arms to her, holding her tightly and rocking her gently against his body as he comforted her, gruffly telling her, 'At least we know he's alive...'

'For now,' Georgia agreed with a small shiver. 'If another farmer—'

'Don't worry,' Piers reassured her. 'The police are arranging to put out a bulletin on the local radio network about Ben.'

As Georgia moved in his arms, lifting her face up to his so that she could listen to him, the temptation to cup it in his hands and kiss the tremble from her mouth was so strong that he had to avert his head and look away from her to stop himself from giving in to it. Ben's plight had united them, locking them together in an enclosed and intimate circle of mutual concern for the dog, but he must not deceive himself. Once the situation had been resolved Georgia would, no doubt, return to her uncompromising stand of antipathy towards him. Just because last night she had seemed to welcome him, to *want* him...

'How soon can we leave? How long will it take us to get there?' he heard her asking him anxiously.

'Well, it could be a three- or four-hour drive, depend-

ing on road conditions. We'll have to take my godmother's car and—'

'We could take mine,' Georgia offered.

Piers shook his head, reminding her truthfully, 'My
godmother's Volvo has more room for Ben.'

'If we find him…' Georgia couldn't prevent herself
from pointing out.

'If we find him,' Piers agreed. 'By the way,' he
added, 'it might be as well to pack an overnight bag.
We shan't get to the farm until early evening, and even
with the benefit of the light summer nights we could—'

'If Ben is up there I'm not coming back without him,'
Georgia told Piers determinedly. 'No matter *how* long I
have to stay. Oh, Piers, what on earth will we tell your
godmother?' she asked him unhappily.

'Let's cross that bridge when we get to it,' Piers told
her quietly. 'Whilst you're getting ready I'll go and fill
the Volvo with petrol.'

As he started to release her Georgia turned away from
him, but then, as all her doubts and fears swept over
her, she turned back.

'Piers…'

The husky, anxious note of her voice made Piers jerk
his head round to look at her. Her mouth was within
easy kissing distance of his own. Recklessly he ignored
the stern voice admonishing him not to give in to his
longing, sliding his hand along her jaw and then bending
his head to take her mouth in a swift, hard kiss.

As he felt her lips tremble and then part beneath his,
momentarily Piers forgot Ben and everything else that
lay between them, keeping them apart. Very gently his
tonguetip probed Georgia's soft lips even further apart,
the tremble that ran through her body echoed by the
deep shudder of arousal racking his own.

Dizzily Georgia clung to Piers as his tongue explored the deep sweetness of her mouth, taking possession of it with a determined sensuality that both shocked and thrilled her.

She loved him so much. If only there weren't all these barriers between them. If only his desire for her was motivated by love and not merely male physical hunger.

Pain tore through her, causing her to give a small, anguished sob. Immediately Piers released her, and, his voice gruff and deep, his glance fixed somewhere in the distance, told her almost curtly, 'I'm sorry. I didn't—'

'I'll go and pack my bag,' Georgia interrupted him.

Highly emotive situations often resulted in people behaving in a way that was out of character. Piers felt guilty about Ben and that was why he was behaving as he was towards her, she told herself sternly as she made her way upstairs.

Mrs Latham's sturdy Volvo might be nowhere as luxurious as Piers's Jaguar, with its leather upholstery and elegant interior, but it was way superior to her own runabout, Georgia acknowledged.

They had made good time on the motorway; Piers was an excellent driver and Georgia knew that, had the circumstances been different, right now she would have been awed and thrilled by the views outside the car windows as they drove through the Yorkshire Dales, with their vast sweeps of hillside and sky. The last village they had driven through had been small and pretty, with its stone cottages clinging to the banks of a crystal-clear river.

Piers had offered to stop, suggesting that Georgia might want to have something to eat and stretch her legs, but she had shaken her head, despite the fact that the only food she had had all day had been the piece of toast she had managed to force down at breakfast. She just wasn't hungry. Anxiety gnawed at her stomach with sharply painful teeth, and the rolling hills of the Dales, bare apart from their flocks of sheep, which at any other time would have excited her admiration, right now only reinforced how empty and vast the area was, and how ill equipped a town-reared, pampered dog like Ben was to survive in such rugged terrain.

Despite Piers's skilled driving it was almost four hours after they had left before they were bumping down the narrow lane that led to the Bowleses' farm.

Anxiously Georgia scanned the skyline, hoping against hope to see Ben, and her first words as Piers stopped his godmother's car in the yard and Mrs Bowles came hurrying out to greet them were, 'Has Ben—? Have you—?'

'No sight of him, I'm afraid,' Mary Bowles told Georgia, adding to Piers, 'If you wouldn't mind parking your car in the empty barn at the bottom of the yard? That will leave room for Harry to turn the tractor when he comes in.

'Come on inside,' she invited Georgia, who had stopped to talk to the farm collie, who, much to Mary Bowles's surprise, had actually allowed Georgia to stroke her.

'You're honoured,' she told Georgia as she ushered her into the kitchen. 'Meg doesn't normally take to strangers.'

Jack, the mixed breed, extricated himself from his basket beside the old-fashioned Aga as they walked in. He was stiff and rheumatic and Georgia automatically checked his swollen joints as she stroked him.

'Habit,' she told Mary Bowles, who was watching her, and explained how she earned her living.

'Best not tell Harry that,' Mary counselled her with a laugh. 'He'll have you out on the hill looking at his precious sheep before you can turn round if you do!'

'The police said that your husband thought Ben had been worrying his flock,' Georgia responded unhappily.

'Well, something has been at the lambs. It might have been the dog, but it could as easily have been a fox,' Mary told her calmly.

'He won't... He wouldn't...' Georgia began huskily, unable to put into words her dread that Ben might be shot as a sheep-worrier before they could find him. But before she could vocalise her fears Piers came into the kitchen.

'We thought, with your husband's permission, that we'd go out ourselves and look for Ben,' Piers informed Mary Bowles after he had accepted her offer of a cup of tea. 'He'll recognise both our voices, but especially Georgia's, and if he is here the sound of a familiar voice might persuade him to come out of hiding.'

'Oh, he certainly was here,' Mary insisted. 'I saw him myself...fed him... Nice-looking dog...

'Yes, that's definitely the dog I saw,' she confirmed as Piers produced a photograph of Ben which Georgia realised he must have found amongst his godmother's belongings.

'Well, you won't be the only ones looking for him,' she told Georgia and Piers with a chuckle. 'They've been giving it out on the radio all day that there's a reward for his safe return.'

'Good. The more people looking for him the better,' Piers replied.

'I thought he might have come down off the hill when

I fed Meg and Jack again,' Mary Bowles admitted. 'I even left an extra bowl of food out just in case, but there was no sign of him.'

They had to wait half an hour for Harry Bowles to come in so that he could take them up on to the hill to show them just where he had seen Ben.

Cupping her hands together, Georgia called his name, the sound bouncing back to her and sending some nearby sheep scurrying fleet-footedly away. A narrow sheep track wound up across the hill, disappearing into the distance.

'Perhaps if we follow the track calling his name?' Piers suggested.

Nodding in acquiescence, Georgia fell into step beside him, leaving Harry Bowles to return to his farming duties.

'Why didn't he just stay at the farm?' Georgia almost wept an hour later as she crested yet another hill without any sight of Ben.

'Ben...' she shouted. 'Ben...'

'We'll have to start making tracks back to the farm,' Piers warned her. 'The light's already starting to fade.'

Georgia wanted to protest, but her common sense warned her that he was right.

Back in the farmhouse kitchen Georgia wearily accepted the fresh cup of tea Mary Bowles offered her. She was beginning to feel the effects of the previous night's loss of sleep, her body heavy and tired, but her thoughts, her mind, were almost too alert, as though they had gone into overdrive. Over and over again she kept visualising Ben on his own on the hillside and all the dangers he would be exposed to. Her eyelids felt so heavy; perhaps if she just closed her eyes for a moment...

'We're going to need to stay overnight,' Piers told Mary Bowles softly. 'Is there somewhere locally you could recommend?'

'As I mentioned over the phone earlier, you're more than welcome to stay here,' Mary returned promptly.

She shook her head when Piers protested that they didn't want to cause her any trouble, informing him firmly, 'It will be no trouble at all. We sometimes get walkers asking for a room, and there's a spare bed already made up. You and your wife would be more than welcome to it.'

You and your wife! Piers opened his mouth to inform Mary that he and Georgia weren't even a couple, never mind man and wife, and that there was no way Georgia would want to share a bed with him, but before he could say anything Mary was looking indulgently towards Georgia, who had fallen asleep in her chair.

She said softly, 'Poor girl, she's worn out. I'll take you up and show you the room. We don't keep late hours as Harry likes to be up at dawn.'

As Piers followed Mary Bowles up the narrow, winding flight of stairs that led to the farm's upper storey, he told himself that there was no point in complicating the issue at this stage by informing her that he and Georgia weren't married. It was gone ten in the evening, and by the time he had woken Georgia up and they had driven back to the small market town they had passed on the way to the farm it would be close on midnight before they found anywhere to stay—if they could find anywhere! Far easier simply to accept Mary's offer.

The room Mary showed him wasn't particularly large, but it was spotlessly clean and comfortably furnished and it had its own shower room.

'We had that put in when our daughter was growing

up. Teenage girls like to spend a lot of time in the bathroom, and her dad got that impatient with her. She's at university now.' She gave a small sigh, and Piers could see from her face that she missed her daughter.

As they walked back into the kitchen Georgia woke up and said anxiously to Piers, 'We need to sort out somewhere to stay.'

'It's all arranged,' Piers told her. 'Mrs Bowles has offered to put us up here.'

Georgia's expression betrayed her relief, and Piers suspected that she was as loath as he had been himself to drive back into the nearest town to find somewhere to stay. He would have to wait until they were on their own to explain Mary Bowles's incorrect assumption that they were married, and to assure Georgia that the fact that they were having to share a room and a bed did not mean that she need have any fear that he would attempt to take advantage of their imaginary status.

'Oh, that is kind of you,' Georgia told the farmer's wife, confirming Piers's thought as she continued, 'I must admit I wasn't looking forward to having to get back in the car. I thought I was a good walker, but these hills have really tired me out.'

'They're steeper than they look,' Mary Bowles agreed with a smile, continuing, 'I'll make us all a spot of supper, and then Harry and I will be off to our bed.

'Try not to worry about the dog,' she told Georgia gently. 'Brian—that's my brother—is in the police, and he's promised to let us know the moment they hear anything.'

'We'll say goodnight, then,' Mary Bowles told Georgia after the two of them had finished clearing up from the hearty supper she had given them.

As they heard the couple's footsteps on the stairs Georgia smothered a yawn and looked tiredly at Piers.

'I think I'll go up as well,' she told him. 'Which room?'

'I'll come with you and show you,' Piers offered.

Nodding, Georgia followed him as he led the way towards the stairs.

Piers waited until they were both in the room with the door safely closed before breaking the news to her.

'We're *what*?' Georgia demanded, shaking her head as she told him fiercely, 'Oh, no; no way am I sharing a room, never mind a *bed* with you.'

'Shush. Keep your voice down,' Piers warned her. 'Mary Bowles thinks we're a married couple. That's why she's put us both in here.'

'Why didn't you tell her that we aren't?' Georgia demanded angrily.

'I intended to at first, but then I realised she probably only had one room ready for guests. She's a farmer's wife, Georgia; I doubt she's got enough spare time to start making up another guest bedroom. You heard her this evening when she was talking about her life; when she isn't rearing orphan lambs and feeding hens and ducks, she's working in her vegetable garden or making jams and chutneys. By the sound of it she never has a second to spare. What was I supposed to do—wake you up and drag you on a long drive into the nearest town and then trail you round its streets whilst we searched for somewhere to stay?'

Georgia grimaced, a fresh wave of tiredness hitting her.

'Look, if it makes you feel any better, I'll sleep in the chair or on the floor,' Piers offered grimly.

Georgia looked at the small nursing chair and then at

the floor. There was no way *she* would have wanted to sleep on either of them.

'You should have told her,' was all she could bring herself to say as she looked away from Piers. The stress of the last twenty-four hours was beginning to take its toll; her eyes felt gritty with exhaustion. She was too tired to argue with Piers. All she wanted to do was go to bed and sleep. No, she corrected herself wearily, all she really wanted to do was to find Ben. At least if they stayed here at the farm they would be on the spot to make a fresh search for him first thing in the morning.

'There's a shower room through there,' Piers told her, sensing her mood. 'You can use it first.'

'My bag with my overnight things is still in the car,' Georgia reminded him.

'Yes, so's mine,' Piers agreed. 'I'll go down and get them.'

Whilst he was gone Georgia showered quickly, wrapping her damp body in one of the plain clean towels Mary Bowles had provided.

From the bedroom window she could look down into the farmyard, and she paused in the act of closing the curtains. Where was Ben? Could he see the farm...could he see the yard...had he heard them calling but perhaps been too afraid to show himself to them?

Anxiously she stared out into the darkness, not hearing and unaware of Piers's return until his brief touch on her arm made her spin round in shock.

'Sorry,' he apologised as he saw her startled expression. 'I thought you'd heard me come in.'

'I was thinking about Ben,' Georgia told him in a stifled voice. He was standing far too close to her—so close that she almost felt imprisoned between him and the wall—but it wasn't fear of that imprisonment that was making her heart start to pound so heavily and her body start to tremble, nor were the thoughts or the images which were filling her mind now of the dog. The heaviness which was filling her body now had nothing whatsoever to do with tiredness or a need for sleep. Far from it. The need pounding through her as swiftly as sand in a timer sprang from a far more dangerous source.

Piers could feel his body reacting to Georgia's closeness. She looked so unbearably desirable, so heart-wrenchingly lovable, he wanted to take her in his arms right there and...

Unable to stem the words, he began urgently, 'Georgia, about last night...'

This was it; Piers was going to tell her not to read the wrong message into what had happened between them last night.

Frantically she shook her head. There were some things she just didn't want to hear, some truths she couldn't bear to endure. Not now.

'I don't want to talk about it,' she told Piers fiercely. 'Where have you put my things?'

'Your bag is over there,' Piers told her, gesturing towards the foot of the bed. As he turned his head Georgia squeezed past him, scarcely daring to breathe in case in doing so she inadvertently allowed her body to touch his; her starving loving senses could only endure so much!

Seeing the look of intensity on her face as she squeezed past him, as though loathing the very thought of touching him, Piers felt the pain of her rejection as sharply as though she had knifed him through his heart. In bed last night he had warned himself against reading anything into her responsiveness to him, but it seemed he had not listened to his own advice. Not daring to allow himself to look at her again, he strode towards the shower room.

Even with her back to him Georgia was acutely aware of him, waiting until she had heard the shower-room door close behind him before reaching into her holdall and hastily removing her damp towel to scramble into the cotton nightdress she had brought with her whilst Piers was safely out of the way.

That done, she clambered quickly into the old-fashioned high-framed bed, determinedly closing her eyes and pulling the covers up high around her ears, willing herself to fall asleep before Piers came back into the bedroom.

She almost was, and in fact she was sure that she would have been if Piers hadn't lingered so long in the shower room that she grew tense and wakeful listening for him.

Surely Georgia must be asleep by now? Piers decided as he cautiously opened the shower-room door and walked towards the bed. Georgia was lying facing away from the centre of the bed, her body completely still.

A little ruefully Piers looked at her, and then at his own robe-clad body. He hadn't worn pyjamas since he had left home to go to university and didn't, in fact, possess a pair, but he could well imagine Georgia's likely reaction if he were to go to bed nude, which meant that he would have to sleep in his robe or risk her condemnation. The bedroom was low-ceilinged and warm, even with the window open, but, tempted though he was to dispense with the unwanted insulation of his heavy towelling robe, he judged that it would not be a good idea to do so.

Sighing faintly, he pushed back the bedclothes and got into bed.

Piers was in bed with her. A delicious shiver ran right through Georgia's body, bringing her out in a rash of sensually sensitive goosebumps.

A *delicious* shiver? Sternly she warned her thoughts not to even think about tempting her or tormenting her with the silken web of alluring sensuality they were attempting to weave around her, shadowy images of Piers, his body nakedly warm and welcoming, enticing her fingers to explore its every line and plane, his arms wrapping tightly around her, his throat stretching with the urgency of the low groan he made as his need for her overwhelmed him.

Frantically Georgia squeezed her eyes as tightly closed as she could, reminding herself of just how tired she was and of exactly why they were here. It was Ben that she ought to be concentrating on. Where was he? *How* was he? Ben… Determinedly she forced herself to visualise the dog. Ben…

Ben sniffed the night air. Out there in the small, protected valley enclosed by the hills he could smell his evening meal. He licked his lips, anticipating the rich taste of fresh meat. A river ran through the valley, which was why he had come here in the first place, thirsty after his day spent searching for food.

He had been watching his quarry for several hours now. Had seen them arrive and had known that he would have to be patient, waiting until he could do what he knew he had to do under the cover of darkness.

It *was* dark now, his quarry merely unmoving shapes against the darkness of the hillside.

Stealthily Ben made his way down towards them, crouching on his belly, ears and eyes stretched for any sound that would warn him that they had sensed him coming.

But nothing moved.

Ben knew exactly where he had to go. He had not spent the afternoon watching the Cub Scouts making camp for nothing. He knew exactly which tent housed those delicious-looking and even more delicious-smelling sausages he had seen being unpacked. Ben loved sausages. Mrs Latham's butcher made his own, and she often allowed Ben one for a Sunday morning treat.

'This is *our* secret, Ben,' she'd often told him. *Sausages!* Ben could smell them now. Breathing deeply, he sniffed the air appreciatively.

Until he had seen the Cubs making camp he had thought that he would have to go back to the farm and run the gauntlet not just of the farmer's gun but of the collie's hostility into the bargain. The bark and growl she had given him had made it perfectly clear that she did not consider him to be a welcome visitor.

Glancing over his shoulder, Ben checked that nothing and no one was watching him before sneaking into the tent where the scout master had carefully stored his troop's food. This was an annual trip to this secluded camping spot, and one which the younger boys always thoroughly enjoyed.

The sausages were in the Calor gas fridge, but the fridge was no deterrent to Ben, who had long ago worked out how such things could be opened. Deftly he opened this one...

CHAPTER NINE

PIERS was dreaming about Ben. He had taken the dog for a walk and Ben had brought a stick for Piers to throw, dropping it at his feet. As Piers picked up the stick and threw it across what he had thought to be a vast open expanse of empty countryside, the countryside transformed itself into a hideously busy six-lane motorway.

Piers opened his mouth to warn Ben not to run after the stick, but it was too late: the dog was already racing towards the motorway and certain destruction.

Despairingly Piers called the dog's name.

At first when she heard Piers calling out Ben's name, Georgia, still half asleep, imagined that he must have somehow spotted the dog, but when she looked automatically towards the bedroom window Piers wasn't standing there and the curtains were closed.

Fully awake now, she sat up in bed, switching on the bedside lamp.

Piers was lying in bed beside her, obviously in the grip of a nightmare, his forehead beaded with sweat as he lunged to the other side of the bed as though trying to catch hold of something or someone.

'Piers…' Instinctively Georgia reached over to him, reaching for his shoulder and shaking him.

'Piers,' she repeated a little more anxiously as she heard him whispering brokenly,

'Ben… No… Please, no…' His voice was raw with pain and guilt.

As she shook him a little harder his eyes opened, and she could see quite clearly in them his anguish and guilt.

'Georgia?' He looked at her in confusion, frowning as he turned his head and stared round the farmhouse bedroom.

'It's all right,' Georgia reassured him gently. 'You were having a dream.'

'A nightmare,' Piers corrected her tersely, sitting up in the bed and pushing his hand through his hair as he came fully awake.

'You called out Ben's name,' Georgia told him sombrely. 'At first I thought you must have seen him, but then I realised that you were still asleep.'

As he had sat up in bed Georgia had seen that he was wearing a thick towelling robe, but he must have left it unfastened, she recognised, because as he turned towards her it gaped open, revealing the bronze breadth of his chest.

Was it really only last night that she had…? The sudden surge of heat that hit her made her look away from him, biting sharply on her bottom lip as she tried to suppress her reaction to him.

'Don't *do* that,' she heard Piers begging her huskily.

'What?' she asked him in confusion, releasing her lip and looking automatically back at him.

'That,' Piers told her, touching the spot on her lip where the impact of her teeth had left a small, tender swelling.

The unexpected sensuality of his fingertip brushing against her lip was heart-stoppingly intimate.

'Why…why shouldn't I do it?' she managed to ask

him shakily as she felt his burning gaze slide over her skin.

'Because it makes *me* want to do *this*,' Piers told her in a thick voice that had the same effect on her senses as if she were being licked by the rough tongue of a tiger.

Her body completely still, Georgia watched the descent of Piers's mouth, knowing what was going to happen even before she felt the velvety, hot stroke of his mouth caressing her own. Helplessly she closed her eyes, and then opened them again in deprivation as Piers lifted his mouth from hers.

'I would never have hurt Ben,' he told her rawly. 'I want you to believe that, Georgia. I may not have thought he was a suitable pet for my godmother but I never...' He stopped and shook his head. 'I should never have put him in the car. I should have brought him back to you before going to see the estate agent. I wish to God I had,' he told her vehemently. 'Because then he would have been safe.'

'As I've tried to reassure you before, it isn't your fault,' Georgia said, but Piers shook his head.

'Neither of us believes that,' he told her grimly.

To her own surprise Georgia heard herself not just saying but meaning as well, '*I* believe it, Piers.'

'You're so sweet,' she heard him telling her thickly. 'So sweet and so...'

Georgia shuddered in delight as his mouth opened over hers in a kiss of fierce passion and promise. She wanted to tell Piers that he must stop what he was doing, that he mustn't encourage her to betray herself and her love to him by kissing her the way he was doing, but somehow the words were never uttered. Instead, she was clinging to him, wrapping her arms around his neck as she opened her mouth to his kiss, seeking, finding and claiming the hot thrust of his tongue with a female urgency that made Piers stiffen and then shudder.

Wrenching his mouth away from hers, he told her rawly, 'If you keep on kissing me like that there's no way I'm going to be able to stay here in this bed with you and not give you with my body what you're asking me for with your mouth.'

For a moment Georgia was too shocked to say anything, heat scalding her skin as she took in the full meaning of what he was saying. In the lamplight she could see the hot sheen of his torso.

'I...I wasn't asking for anything,' she denied huskily, but she couldn't quite bring herself to look into Piers's eyes, and she knew that the little tremors of sensation thrilling through her body were making a mockery of her verbal denial.

'Weren't you?' Piers countered swiftly. 'Come here and prove it to me, then, Georgia; come here and lie next to me, skin against skin, heartbeat against heartbeat, and tell me again that you don't want me. That this...' he paused as his fingertip delicately touched the place where the frantic betraying pulse thudded at the base of her throat '...doesn't mean what we both know it does...'

Very deliberately he slipped the straps of her nightdress down off her shoulders so that it fell free of her immobile body, revealing the full curves of her breasts. Even more delicately he touched her nipples—so tautly erect and sensitive to him that Georgia shuddered visibly in reaction as he did so.

'Oh, God, you don't know what it does to me to see you reacting to me like that,' she heard Piers telling her thickly. 'You *want* me to touch you, Georgia...to hold

you…taste you…' His voice was so thickly muffled that
Georgia could barely hear what he was saying—or was
it because her own heart was beating so loudly and so
fast that she wasn't sure whether or not he had said that
final, fatal 'You want me to love you' or not?

And anyway, what did it matter what he had said, or
what he had guessed? What did anything matter now
other than the aching need that filled her? A woman's
need, driven by a woman's love; her body was so ready
for him, so longing for him, so empty for him.

Proudly Georgia arched her back as his hands held
and shaped her breasts, her eyes heavy-lidded with passion as she watched his head bend towards her body.

A tiny shocked gasp of pleasure quivered past her lips
as he began to explore one taut nipple delicately with
his mouth. The most exquisitely arousing sensation shot
through her, quicksilver, mercurial rivulets of pleasure
that had her writhing in sensual torment against him.

Just for one brief second reality slipped through the
rainbow-coloured delight she was experiencing.

'No!' she protested muzzily as Piers pushed the bedclothes aside and slid her nightdress completely free of
her body at the same time as he removed his own robe.
The reality of him was so much more than she had
imagined, so powerfully, awesomely male.

'No,' she whispered. 'We shouldn't…we mustn't…
Without love…'

'You mustn't be ashamed of wanting me,' Piers whispered back. 'Desire isn't wrong, Georgia, it's a normal,
natural human need.'

Perhaps for him it was, Georgia recognised, but for
her…

'Love matters,' she protested fiercely. 'I should… I
need—'

'You need this; you need *me*...' Piers interrupted her softly.

The touch of his hands against her skin was enticing her into a world she couldn't bear to resist, luring her there with a hundred—no, a *thousand* sensual promises she knew he could fulfil. Just the sweep of his hand against her naked flesh as he caressed the length of her spine, just the warmth of his breath against her mouth as he lifted her to his own body and started to kiss her were enough to vanquish all the arguments her inner voice of caution could muster.

And instead of repudiating him she heard herself saying helplessly as he touched her, 'Oh, yes...yes...'

And then she closed her eyes and let him lead her into such an unfamiliar country that to name it merely 'pleasure' was like calling the sun 'warm'.

'Hasn't anyone ever done this for you before?' Piers asked her tenderly at one moment when she was so unable to conceal from him what she was feeling that her eyes actually started to fill with tears, so unbearably intense was her pleasure.

'Wait until I love you there with my mouth,' he whispered slowly to her, watching as the expressions chased one another across her face, wondering if she had any idea how close she brought him to the edge of completion just by the way she was reacting to his words and his touch.

He wanted her more than he had the words to tell her, but out of love for her he wanted to prolong every precious second of this special time with her, not to enhance his own pleasure but to give him enough memories of her to last him through all the long, dark times when she wasn't going to be there.

Her honesty when she had as good as told him that

she couldn't love him and when she had struggled to admit her physical need for him had brought him the closest he had ever come to tears in all his adult life. Without her love this act of intimacy between them should have been shallow and meaningless, but with every breath she took, every look she gave him, every small shudder and sigh what she was doing was deepening his love and his longing for her. She was so natural, so giving, so loving even without loving him, that his self-control reached the point of no return sooner than he would have wished.

Quickly he reached for her, sliding her the length of his body and then kneeling over her as he kissed first her mouth and then her breasts.

He looked, Georgia thought dizzily, like some Greek god of old, and she felt much as she imagined her mythological female counterpart must have done, her body quivering with longing and awe, her emotions bonding her to the magnificent male she knew, in her heart, she could never hold and with whom she could never have more than this one precious, intimate night—a night that would stay in her memory for ever.

Tremulously Georgia reached out and touched him, running her fingertips along his collarbone and then down the length of his body.

'Yes,' Piers urged her thickly when her fingers came to rest in the soft pubic hair that enclosed his maleness. 'Yes,' he repeated rawly. 'Touch me, *know* me, Georgia. I want…' And then, almost before her hesitant fingers had had time to do more than merely sketch the shape and feel of him, he was removing them to ease himself very slowly and carefully inside her.

Each careful movement, each deliberately controlled thrust made her gasp in shocked delight, her body convulsing around him, laying claim to him and welcoming him.

Georgia cried out loud as she felt him reach fulfilment deep within her, the hot burst of his release triggering her own white-lightning explosion of pleasure, starburst after starburst of it until she was shuddering in Piers's arms, crying out his name in between her indrawn gulps of air.

'Piers,' she whispered as the grateful tears of release cooled her heated face.

'Hush,' he soothed her, drawing her as close to his body as he could and holding her there as he stroked her tear-damp face and kissed her mouth gently. 'Don't say anything, Georgia. That was so perfect...so beautiful...so right.'

So right? When he didn't love her? Despite her physical satisfaction Georgia could feel the sharpness of her own pain. But he *was* right about one thing: what was the point in her saying anything? Piers obviously thought her desire for him had been motivated by the same physical need which had driven him, and what was the point in adding to her own misery by telling him the truth?

Hungrily she snuggled closer to him. She needed this intimate contact, this intimate closeness with him so much. Her starved senses ached for it so much. Wearily she closed her eyes.

When she opened her eyes again it was morning. The sun was shining out of an impossibly clear blue sky and Piers was lying in bed next to her. As she looked uncertainly at him, trying not to betray just how potent an effect the sight of his naked torso was having on her, or of the sensual memories it evoked, he moved to her and said softly, 'Hello, you...'

Hello, you! Two very simple words but, oh, what a sense of intimacy, sharing and belonging they conveyed—what a *false* sense of intimacy, sharing and belonging they conveyed, Georgia's aching heart warned her.

Piers felt nothing for her emotionally. She knew that. But she could see he was waiting for her to make some kind of response. Gravely she gave it, returning his greeting with a rather more formal and quiet, 'Hello.'

'Georgia...'

Liquid heat suffused her as her body reacted to the sensual urgency she could hear in Piers's voice when he started to reach for her.

'We ought to get up and start searching for Ben,' Georgia reminded him breathlessly. 'It's a wonderful day...'

'Wonderful,' Piers agreed, showing no sign of doing anything other than tightening his hold on her. 'Wonderful,' he repeated as he feathered the lightest of kisses against her mouth. 'Just like you...'

At the campsite the boys were already awake and clamouring for their breakfast. On the far side of the river Ben waited expectantly as the scent of frying food filled the air. Last night's stolen sausages had tasted very good, but now he was hungry again.

Where the boys were camping the river formed a natural pool, quite deep in places, fed at one end where the hillside fell away to create a natural waterfall, and, as Ben had already discovered, the river was quite fast moving, and only really safe to cross at the furthest end of the small valley.

He headed this way now. Under normal circumstances he would have disdained to touch scraps, his preferred diet being the special food Mrs Latham bought for him plus his extra 'luxury treats'. But right now his mouth was already watering at the thought of the boys' left-over bits of bacon and sausage.

As he padded down towards the shallowest part of the river Ben paused when he heard the boys being summoned for their breakfast. Two of them, either not having heard or deliberately ignoring the summons, were standing on an outcrop of rocks beside one of the deepest parts of the pool, skimming stones across its surface. Ben watched them, and as he did so one of the boys grabbed hold of the other's shirt, shaking him as though warning him that it was time to go, but the other boy shook him off, stepping back from him as he told him that he wasn't ready to go yet.

'We've got to,' his companion protested, trying to take hold of his arm a second time, but as his friend laughed and evaded his grasp tragedy struck and he lost his footing, falling backwards into the deep water.

'Alex!'

As Ben heard the anxiety in the now solitary boy's voice he leapt into immediate action. He wasn't a dog bred specifically to retrieve game from water, but he innately knew what had to be done. Quickly he swam strongly towards the spot where the boy had disappeared beneath the water, quickly finding his inert body.

It wasn't easy getting underneath him and lifting him to the surface, rolling him over on to his back so that he could fasten his teeth into his clothes and tug him back to dry land, but, to Ben's relief, as he stalwartly doggy-paddled to the river bank, determinedly taking his human find with him, other help was at hand.

The other boy had run back to the camp to alert them to what had happened, and now there were many pairs of willing hands to help Ben and to relieve him of the boy.

'Good dog… Oh, *good* dog,' someone was praising him, and on the dry sandy ground beside the river bank the boy was coughing up water and protesting that he was all right.

Shaking the water from his coat, Ben happily accompanied the children, who were coaxing him back to the campsite, even more happily accepting the food they offered him and the praise they heaped on him.

A team of paramedics came to take the now recovered victim of the accident to hospital, 'just as a precaution', and Ben's heroism was again extolled for their benefit.

As he accompanied them to the waiting ambulance the leader of the troop confided to one of the ambulancemen his belief that, without Ben's timely intervention, the outcome of the accident could have been very different and far more grave.

'A setter did you say?' the man questioned the Scout leader, frowning a little as he waited for the man's response.

'Yes, that's right. He's with the children now. A nice dog…friendly…'

'Hmm… Well, there's been a setter reported missing on the local news. Seems like someone must be very anxious to get him back because there's a reward offered for his safe return.'

'And do you think this might be the same dog?'

'Could be. If it is he answers to the name of Ben, and he's got one of those implanted microchip identity tags.'

'Mmm…' Georgia quivered in mute delight as she heard the male pleasure in Piers's voice as his mouth caressed hers. Beneath the bedclothes his hand had found the soft mound of her breast and her nipple was already hardening into excited eagerness at his touch.

'Hello...? I'm sorry to wake you, but...'

'It's Mrs Bowles,' Georgia hissed frantically to Piers as she pulled uncomfortably away from him.

But Piers was already getting out of bed, reaching quickly for his robe, as unfazed by the farmer's wife's urgent knock on the door as she was agitated by it.

'Hang on a sec,' he called out, turning his head to smile reassuringly at Georgia and to check that she was completely composed before going to open the door.

'Sorry to disturb you,' Mary Bowles apologised again, 'but there's been a phone call from my brother about your dog. Seems like—'

'Ben? Someone's seen Ben?' Georgia interrupted her excitedly, forgetting her earlier embarrassment and her self-consciousness as she sat up in the bed, hugging the bedclothes around her naked body. 'What? Where?' she questioned eagerly.

But Piers shook his head to silence her, saying encouragingly to the farmer's wife, 'You say Ben's been found?'

'Seems so,' she agreed, and quickly explained to them both what had happened. 'Anyway, they've got him at the police station in the town now, and you're to go down just as soon as you're ready to identify him. Seems like your dog's a bit of a hero,' she added with a smile. 'I expect the parents of the little boy he saved will certainly think so. Now, if you want me to bring you both up a cup of tea...'

He turned his head to look at Georgia, who, now that her initial relief and excitement were subsiding, was be-

ginning to realise that she was going to have to get out
of bed in front of Piers without any clothes on. The fact
that he had seen, touched, caressed every part of her the
previous night, and would have done so again this morning, in the full light of day, and not just with her agree-
ment but with her encouragement, in no way allayed the
sense of discomfort she felt now.

As though somehow Piers sensed what she was feeling, to Georgia's relief she heard him saying to Mary
Bowles, 'No. There's no need for you to go to so much
trouble. I'll come down with you and make us both a
drink.'

Georgia barely waited until Piers had closed the door
before leaping out of bed and making a dash for the
shower room.

Ten minutes later she was just zipping up her jeans
when Piers walked back in, carrying a tray with two
mugs of hot tea on it and some delicious-smelling pieces
of freshly cooked toast.

'Is it really true? Have they *really* found Ben?'
Georgia questioned him anxiously as he handed her one
of the mugs of tea and offered her the toast.

'It certainly sounds like it. I rang the local police
station whilst I was downstairs and spoke to the sergeant
in charge, and he's confirmed that the dog they've got
there answers Ben's description.'

'Oh, I hope it is,' Georgia told him shakily. 'I've been
dreading having to tell your godmother that—'

'How do you think I've been feeling?' Piers interrupted her wryly. 'Give me five minutes,' he told her,
'and then we'll go.'

Since he had been tactful enough to remove himself
from the room to allow her the privacy in which to get
showered and dressed, it seemed only good manners that

she should return the favour, but, for some reason, Georgia discovered that she was oddly reluctant to do so, almost as though she couldn't bear the thought of being apart from him.

Well, she was going to have to learn to do so, she warned herself sternly. Once they were home...once Mrs Latham was back from holiday...there would be no reason whatsoever for her and Piers to have any kind of contact with one another. And, since she was going to have to learn to live without him, despite her love for him, the best thing she could do was to start right now by sensibly going downstairs to wait for him.

So why wasn't she acting on this eminently sensible advice? Why was she staying where she was, making a long job of drinking her tea and eating her toast whilst she wandered over to the window and stared out of it?

She could hear Piers moving about behind her, and then the shower-room door opened and closed again. Now she really should go downstairs. As she knew from her own experience, the shower room was not large enough for one to get dressed in. Once Piers had showered, when he re-emerged into the bedroom he would not be dressed. He would be... She tensed as the shower-room door opened and she heard Piers asking her casually, 'Georgia, could you just pass me my bag? I left it over there by the window last night and my shaving stuff is in it.'

A little nervously Georgia went to pick up the bag she could see lying only a couple of feet away, carrying it to where Piers stood by the open shower-room door. He had a towel draped round his hips, but that didn't do anything to stop Georgia recognising that beneath it he was naked. His torso and his arms were sleek and slick with moisture, and she knew that beneath the towel his lower body would be the same.

She was aware that her breathing had become audibly erratic, and she could feel hot, self-conscious colour staining her skin as Piers looked at her in amusement and teased, 'What's wrong? Anyone would think you hadn't seen me before...'

'It's not that,' Georgia denied immediately, and then stopped; but it was too late.

'No. I know,' Piers agreed softly, the amusement dying from his eyes to be replaced by something that made her pulse race, her heart beat in triple time with nervous excitement.

'Come here,' he commanded her huskily.

Unable to drag her gaze from his, Georgia did so. Something about the heat, the desire, the need in his eyes was mesmerising her.

When she reached him he took the bag from her and put it down, taking hold of her, his hands on her arms, his thumbs caressing her skin through the fabric of her top. It felt as though he couldn't bear not to touch her, as though he felt compelled to touch her as she felt compelled to be with him.

'What we can both feel, what we both know exists between us, *isn't* something to be ashamed of, you know,' he told her in a deep voice. 'Me wanting you...you wanting me...'

Another minute and she'd be in his arms, and once she was there... Georgia closed her eyes. Her lips ached to press tiny, possessive kisses against his skin, her fingers itched to stroke and explore him, her heart yearned lovingly for him, and every time he touched her it grew harder for her to keep herself from telling him just how she felt...just how much she loved him...

'They'll be waiting for us at the police station,' she reminded him in a stilted voice.

Immediately his hands dropped from her arms.

'Yes. Of course,' he agreed quietly. 'I'd better finish getting dressed.'

'I'll wait for you downstairs,' Georgia told him. This time there was going to be no way she could be tempted to forget the reality of the situation between them. This time she was most definitely going to go downstairs and wait at a safe distance from him.

As Piers heard the bedroom door closing behind Georgia he closed his eyes and thumped his fist against the bedroom wall in self-recrimination. Why on earth had he done that? Why hadn't he just left things as they were instead of trying to force on her emotions that she just didn't want? It was obvious how uncomfortable she felt every time he started to talk about his feelings. He knew enough about women to know that her reaction to him physically wasn't something she was at all familiar with, and he sensed that in the aftermath of their love-making she was even a little uncomfortable about the intimacy they had shared.

He wasn't a vain man, but he couldn't deny how much he had enjoyed knowing, seeing, feeling how completely she was giving herself to him, how totally aroused she was, and how fulfilled their lovemaking had left her. But it still made him ache inside with loss and loneliness to know that she didn't reciprocate his feelings.

Reminding himself that he had only himself to blame for her rejection of him just now, he shaved and dressed quickly. Had Mrs Bowles not interrupted them when she had with the news about Ben, no doubt right this minute he would be lying in bed with Georgia, her body relaxed and love-sated as she lay next to him. Grimly he closed his eyes, reminding himself of the folly of such thoughts.

CHAPTER TEN

GEORGIA looked a little uncertainly at Piers as they pulled up in the car park adjacent to the police station. He had barely spoken to her throughout the drive, and when he had done so his voice had been clipped and curt.

Because he had begun to suspect that her reaction to him in bed might have been caused by something more than mere physical need and he wanted to make it totally plain to her that her love for him was not something he wanted?

Did he think she was so lacking in intelligence, in awareness, that she didn't know that already?

Ignoring the helping hand he was offering her, she got out of the car, thanking him stiffly for opening the door for her.

Side by side and in total silence they walked into the police station, but as Georgia saw Ben lying happily at the side of a large police dog her promise to herself to keep Piers at arm's length was forgotten. Beaming with relief she turned to him and exclaimed, 'It's him! It's Ben!'

As he saw them and recognised them Ben bounded over to them both, his tail wagging as he greeted them.

'Oh, Ben...' Georgia said tearfully, burying her face in his coat to hide her emotional tears.

'No need to ask if this *is* the missing dog,' the desk sergeant chuckled to Piers, who had also, unfathomably, had to reach into his pocket for a handkerchief so that he could blow his nose.

'No,' he agreed huskily, allowing Georgia to finish fussing Ben before he too bent down to stroke the dog.

'Hello, boy,' he greeted him, and a little to Georgia's chagrin Ben immediately ignored her to make a fuss of Piers, almost as though Piers were actually his master.

'I have to tell you that he's going to be something of a hero,' the sergeant told them both once the formalities had been completed. 'The Cub troop have decided that if they are to be allowed to claim the reward you were offering for the dog's return they intend to donate it to local charities, but they also want to nominate Ben for an award for what he did. The parents of the boy he saved have specifically asked us to pass on their thanks to both of you. Without Ben's intervention they feel sure that their son would have been in danger of drowning.

'He's a bit of a character, though, isn't he?' The sergeant laughed. 'We *were* keeping him in the restroom, but he picked up one of the lad's sandwiches and made off with another's trainer, so Titus here has been set to watch over him.'

At the mention of his name the police dog pricked up his ears but remained solidly where he was—on duty!

Georgia gave a faint sigh. She doubted that, no matter how much she tried, Ben could ever be trained to that pitch of immaculate obedience.

'Come on, boy, time to go home,' Piers instructed Ben.

Before they could return, though, they had to call at the farm to thank the Bowleses for their hospitality, and Georgia was amazed when Piers, who had insisted on stopping at a new bookshop on the way back, produced the latest copy of a novel by a well-known writer which he gave to Mrs Bowles as a thank-you.

'Oh, she's one of my favourites, and I haven't got this one!' The farmer's wife beamed as she looked at the cover.

'Yes, I noticed you were a fan of hers,' Piers said, whilst Georgia marvelled both at his powers of observation and his sensitivity. She had been going to suggest that they send Mrs Bowles some flowers.

'It was very thoughtful of you to buy Mrs Bowles a book,' she told him ten minutes later when they were in the Volvo with Ben safely in the back.

'I just happened to notice that she had several of the author's books.' Piers dismissed her praise with a small shrug.

'You're very observant,' Georgia told him colourlessly, and Piers gave her a long, thoughtful look as she turned her head away from him.

'Mmm…well, I'm certainly observant enough to see that there's something wrong. What is it? We've got Ben and—'

'I'm just a bit tired,' Georgia fibbed quickly. How could she tell him that the reason for her misery was the knowledge that in a very few hours' time they would be back at home, and once they were they would be back to their previous relationship? Tonight she wouldn't be spending the night in bed with him. Tomorrow morning he wouldn't be bringing her tea and toast in bed whilst walking semi-naked around the bedroom, tantalising and tormenting her.

'Tired…?' Piers repeated, and then checked as Georgia's face burned a slow, betraying, mortified shade of pink.

The words 'I didn't get much sleep last night' had

been trembling on her lips, but thankfully she had not actually uttered them, even though she could tell what he was thinking even without bringing herself to look directly at him. But to her relief, instead of making any comment, he merely responded, 'Why don't you try to get some sleep whilst I drive back?'

Well, no doubt he would prefer to have her asleep than awake—that way he wouldn't have to bother talking to her. And she imagined that having her asleep was the next best alternative to not having her in the car at all!

Very coolly she told him, 'Yes, I think I will,' and promptly turned her back on him and closed her eyes.

'And the couple whose little boy Ben rescued have nominated him for a "brave dog" award...'

Sipping her tea, Georgia listened patiently whilst Emily Latham talked excitedly about Ben's nomination for the Brave Dog of the Year award.

Emily had returned the previous weekend, leaving Georgia free to return to her own home, and she had not been sorry to do so.

In the remaining time between their own return to Emily Latham's home and her arrival back from her cruise, Georgia doubted that she and Piers had spent more than a handful of minutes together. Not that she was remotely unhappy about that. No, of course she wasn't. Not having to spend time with him had suited her very nicely, thank you...very nicely indeed.

Moreover, she had been more than pleased on her return to work to be told that, because of the interest being shown locally in the pet visits scheme she had inaugurated, Philip had decided that she should be the one to go as an observer on a four-week course being run by a charity that trained dogs to become canine helpers to severely disabled people. Naturally Georgia was thrilled to be offered such an opportunity to observe these dogs going through the final weeks of their training alongside their human partners. One of the dogs and her human counterpart actually lived in the town, and the dog would become one of their potential patients once his own training was over. Georgia knew that it was quite a feather in her cap, professionally speaking, to have received Philip's mark of approval in having been chosen to attend the course.

'Ben is behaving so much better,' Emily Latham enthused as she bent down to pat the dog's head. He was seated at her side and he had greeted Georgia with great enthusiasm on her arrival. Georgia smiled but said nothing. She had a suspicion that part of the reason for Ben's changed behaviour was the effect the traumatic change in his lifestyle had had on him. He was, she believed, more than intelligent enough to have realised now just what a lucky animal he was.

'He has been rather worryingly subdued recently, though,' Emily Latham murmured. 'I was going to bring him into the surgery to be checked over, but Arthur says that he thinks Ben is missing Piers.'

Missing Piers! Georgia tensed, but Emily was getting up out of her chair to answer the doorbell which had just started to ring.

'I'd better go,' Georgia told her quickly, afraid that her hostess's visitor could well be the person she had been at such pains to avoid recently.

'Oh, dear, must you?' Emily fluttered. 'Well, do at least stay to say hello to Arthur, won't you? He told me how fierce you'd been in Ben's defence when he came round to complain about him.'

As she spoke she was hurrying towards the door, her face flushed a very attractive shade of pink, imploring Georgia to stay where she was just for a few minutes.

Obediently Georgia did so, having realised that Emily Latham's visitor could not, as she had dreaded, be Piers, but must instead be the colonel who had called round whilst Emily was away to complain at Ben's desecration of his garden.

'Good afternoon to you, my dear.' The colonel beamed as he followed Emily into her drawing room. 'Delightful to meet you again, and under such auspicious circumstances. Ah…stay, sir…' he commanded Ben, who was about to get up, fixing him with a very stern 'services' stare.

It didn't take long for Georgia to realise that it was more than any mere desire to make sure Ben was behaving himself that had brought the colonel round to see Emily, and Georgia suspected the older woman was by no means indifferent to her ex-military admirer.

Leaving them to enjoy their afternoon tea *à deux*, Georgia drove home.

The four-week training course she was observing began on Monday, and she was going to spend the weekend with her parents before driving straight to the course from her parents' home.

Naturally she was relieved that her visit with Emily Latham had passed without any mention of Piers, and even more relieved that she hadn't had to endure actually seeing him.

But where was he? Emily had said that Ben was missing him. Did that mean he had decided against taking up permanent residence in the town? Had he perhaps decided to move somewhere else? Somewhere as far away from her and her unwanted love as he could possibly get? Well, if so, he needn't have troubled himself. There was no way she was going to make a fool of herself over a man who didn't want her. What did he think she was going to do? Fling herself at his feet and beg him...?

Angry colour scalded her skin. Did he really think that just because she had not been able to control her longing for him, her *love* for him, once, that meant...? Once? a sharply clear inner voice demanded delicately. Her face burning even more hotly, Georgia compressed her mouth and started to make mental lists of everything she had to do before she started her journey to her parents' home.

It was the town's evening rush hour, and a Friday as well, and the traffic was at a standstill, gridlocked, but Georgia valiantly refused to give in to the temptation to allow her thoughts to double-back to Piers.

She would need to pack clothes for the weekend, and for the course she was attending. She had warned her neighbours and her landlord that she would be away. She had put batteries in her small tape recorder so that she could make notes of what she saw. She had checked up on the progress of her patients. She had operated on two dogs and a cat earlier in the day, all three minor procedures, which had come through without any complications, the animals having been reunited with their grateful owners before she had left work.

She had bought her father a copy of a new political biography which she knew he would enjoy for his upcoming birthday, and she had treated her mother and herself to a video of one of their favourite Jane Austen books. She still had to fill her car with petrol and—

Abruptly Georgia tensed as she saw Piers's familiar figure emerging from the local estate agent's office.

Had he been in there to tell them that he wasn't now interested in any local property?

Greedily Georgia absorbed every detail of him: the thickness of his hair and the way it grew down into the nape of his neck, the tanned column of his throat, exposed by the casual shirt he was wearing, its short sleeves revealing the strong muscles of his arms, the late afternoon sunshine glinting on the fine, silky hairs that covered them.

He was close enough for her to be able to see the way he was frowning, as though deep in thought. A pretty girl emerged from a shop next door to the estate agent's, almost bumping into him, and his frown changed to a warm smile as she apologised to him.

The warmth of that smile pierced Georgia's heart. Jealousy was a red-hot burning coal inside her body, a fierce anguish that shocked and hurt her. Determinedly she averted her face, unable to endure looking at them. What if Piers was suggesting that as recompense for bumping into him the girl allowed him to take her for a drink? What if she accepted, smiling another flirtatious smile at him? Georgia could all too easily imagine how tempted she would be, how tantalised at the thought of attracting the interest of a man as good-looking as Piers.

The car in front of her moved off, but Georgia didn't notice. She was too entrapped in the horrible mental images tormenting her. Piers and the pretty girl…a bride and groom looking adoringly into one another's eyes…looking lovingly…

Georgia jumped as the driver behind her sounded his horn, and Piers, alone now, now that the girl who had walked into him had gone on her way, looked over to see what all the commotion was about, his body tensing as he saw Georgia.

He had done everything he could to get her out of his mind…and out of his heart… Those remaining days they had shared together at his godmother's house had been sheer purgatory for him, and, even now, he had no idea just how he'd managed to stop himself from going into Georgia's bedroom and pleading with her to at least *try* to love him. But somehow he had.

He had told himself that it was the best possible thing that could have happened, for both their sakes, when his godmother had returned home and Georgia had moved out, but there wasn't a day that went by without him thinking about her, longing for her. A *day*! He was lucky to make it through an hour, a *minute*, without aching for her, he told himself bitterly.

'Georgia?' He had called her name and started to cross the road to her before he could stop himself.

In her car Georgia was uncomfortably aware of the displeasure of the drivers behind her. Hot-faced, she changed gear, refusing to give in to the temptation to look back across the road to see if Piers was still there…with that oh, so pretty girl…but as the traffic started to move forward she couldn't quite prevent herself from stealing a glance in her driving mirror. Piers was crossing the road behind her but there was no sign of the girl. Perhaps she had rushed home to change for her date with him, Georgia decided forlornly. Oh, how she envied her. Oh, how she wished that things could have been different and that Piers could have loved *her*.

Really, some people had no idea when they were well off, Georgia told herself sternly. She had just returned home from a most enjoyable and informative month spent witnessing the strength and bravery of the people who had been learning how to get the best out of their new canine helpers, and into the bargain she had been invited out by one of the course instructors who, flatteringly, had made it plain that he was attracted to her.

On her return Philip had summoned her into his office and told her how pleased he was with her work and how much he hoped she would stay on with them after her trial period was up, and, despite her gentle refusal of his invitation, the course instructor had telephoned her once she got home, trying to coax her to change her mind.

Yes, she had every reason to feel good about herself and her life. Every reason bar one, that was!

She had arrived back in town early the previous day and had called in to the practice in the afternoon to check in there. Today was her day off and she had done some essential food shopping and all the washing she had brought back from the course with her; she was planning to spend the afternoon indulging in a leisurely walk along the river bank, enjoying the warmth of the summer sun.

And when she did so she was *not* going to think about Piers once. Just as she hadn't thought about him once when she had been away? she taunted herself grimly. Not once, no…just every single day, every single minute!

A couple of hours later, as she was walking along the river path, Georgia heard her name being called by Emily Latham. As she looked towards the older woman she was relieved to see that Piers wasn't with her. The colonel was, though, his manner towards his companion both proprietorial and protective, Georgia noticed when they came over to talk to her.

'Where's Ben?' she asked the older woman conversationally.

'Oh, didn't you know? He doesn't live with me any more,' Emily Latham told her.

'You've re-homed him?' Georgia couldn't keep the distress out of her voice. 'Oh, poor Ben.'

'Oh, no, he's very happy,' Emily told her immediately, 'and Piers was so adamant that it was the right thing to do.'

Piers!

She might have *known*, Georgia realised. Everything he had said to her about him feeling guilty about the way he had been with Ben had simply been a lie. He had quite plainly been planning to get rid of Ben all along, just as he had warned her. And now, it seemed, he had succeeded. Why had she been naive enough to assume that he had changed his mind?

'Yes, we've just been to visit him,' the colonel boomed. 'Can't really understand why a single chap should move into a place as large as his...'

'Piers has bought Riversreach Farm,' Emily informed Georgia happily. 'He moved in just a short time ago.'

Riversreach Farm. Georgia knew it. It was a lovely Georgian farmhouse just outside the town. She had visited the previous owners to look at a cat they had which had gone down with feline flu.

'I do miss Ben,' Emily was saying, 'but Arthur has suggested that I should think about getting a smaller, quieter dog.'

'Where *is* Ben?' Georgia wanted to ask her, but her throat felt too choked with her anger for her to formulate the words. She was surprised that Emily could discuss Ben's banishment with such equanimity. She had seemed so devoted to him. But no doubt Piers had spun her some tale about it being in Ben's interest for him to be re-homed and Emily was naive enough to believe him…just as *she* had done!

Her pleasure in walking totally spoiled, Georgia returned home, but once there she couldn't get poor Ben or his fate out of her mind, and the more she thought about what Piers had done, the angrier she got. It was high time that someone confronted Piers and made him see just how callous and cruel his behaviour was. And who better than she! Who better indeed?

In a trice Georgia was in her car and driving out of the town in the direction of Riversreach Farm.

A 'For Sale' sign still marked the entrance to the farm lane, but the forlorn appearance Georgia remembered the farm as having was well on the way to being banished, she recognised as she reached the end of the lane and saw the house's sparkling windows, their stone surrounds picked out in a buttery cream paint whilst the façade of the house itself had been painted a paler-toned warm cream. The garden at the front of the house had been tidied up as well, the borders weeded and the gravel recently raked. Quite plainly Piers intended to spare no expense in setting the farmhouse to rights, Georgia decided sourly. Pity that he hadn't had the compassion to spend some of his money on doing something for Ben.

Stopping her car, she took a deep breath and pushed open the driver's door.

She wasn't going to let herself dwell on how much of her anger was fuelled by disappointment at what Piers had done, because he had fallen so far short of the ideals of the man she had allowed herself to believe he could be—a man big enough, wise enough, man enough to admit that he had made an error of judgement and that he had been wrong. A man compassionate enough to understand the effect Ben's being found another home, being rejected a second time, might have on the animal; a man caring enough to realise what it must be like for the woman who was foolish enough to love him when he wasn't able to love her back.

But Piers was none of those things. Piers was...

Raising her hand, she was just about to ring the door-bell, but Piers had obviously seen her arrive, because before she could do so he had opened the door and he was standing there.

'Georgia!'

Georgia blinked a little as she heard the warmth in his voice, and then told herself that she must have been imagining it as she ignored his greeting and told him bitterly, 'I know. I've just seen your godmother. I know what's happened to Ben... How could you...? And to think I really believed all those things you said. To think I believed that you'd actually changed your mind about him.

'Have you no feelings, no compassion? No, of course you haven't.' She answered her own question. 'You just couldn't wait to get rid of him, could you? You just couldn't wait to persuade your godmother to find him another home.' Tears filled her eyes. 'And to think I thought you'd changed—'

'Now just a minute,' Piers interrupted her grimly. 'You don't—'

'I don't what? Understand?' Georgia demanded furiously. 'No, I don't. I *don't* understand how any-one...*any* man...could behave towards a dumb animal the way you have to Ben. And to think that I actually believed I loved you...that I've just spent night after night longing for you...wishing you were with me...

wishing that you loved me—' Abruptly Georgia realised what she was saying and where the hot dam-burst of her anger had taken her.

Her face burned, but she lifted her head proudly and locked her eyes on Piers's as she told him quietly, 'You aren't worthy of my love, and I'm glad that I discovered the truth about you before I wasted any more tears on you. Where *is* Ben? I want to know because…'

Her voice trailed away as Piers stepped back into the hall and called, 'Ben, come here. You've got a visitor…'

As the setter came bounding into the hall Georgia couldn't help noticing how happy and healthy he looked. His coat gleamed, his eyes shone and he had that air about him that said that he was getting far more exercise than he had ever done with Emily Latham.

'B-Ben's *here*…?' To her chagrin Georgia knew she was beginning to stammer. 'B-but…'

As the setter rushed up to greet her Georgia kneeled down to pat him, burying her hot face in his coat.

'When the time came for me to move out of my godmother's house and into this one I decided that I really missed Ben, so I asked her if she would consider allowing him to live with me full-time. She was reluctant at first, but the colonel persuaded her; since I suspect any day now that the colonel will propose to her—it's obvious just how the pair of them feel about one another. In the end she agreed that Ben could come to me, with the proviso that, should Ben be in the least bit distressed or unhappy, she would have him back.'

'In the event he's settled down here better than I could have hoped for—haven't you, boy?' Piers asked Ben, reaching out to stroke his ears.

Georgia could see immediately from the way Ben reacted to Piers just how happy the dog was with his new home *and* his new master.

'I...I'm sorry...' Georgia apologised stiltedly as she stood up. 'I didn't realise. I shouldn't have said what I did. I...I must go.' She was practically gabbling as she turned away, ready to make an undignified, hasty dash to her car.

What on earth had prompted her to say the things she had? Bad enough for her to have criticised Piers and accused him so unjustifiably, but to have told him about her own feelings...to have betrayed her unwanted love to him...

'Oh, no, you don't,' Piers told her softly. 'Not yet. You and I have—'

'No, I'm not staying; you can't make me,' Georgia protested apprehensively, quickly moving out of his reach.

But to her consternation, as she started to turn away, Piers said firmly, 'Ben, guard...'

Ben immediately came and stood in front of her. When she tried to get past him the dog caught hold of her wrist in his mouth—very gently, but very determinedly.

Wildly Georgia stared at Piers.

'You *did* say that he was very intelligent,' Piers reminded her dryly, 'and I have to confess that you were right!'

'You can't do this. Make him let me go,' Georgia demanded.

'Not until you agree to come inside and talk to me,' Piers told her.

'We don't have anything to talk about,' Georgia told him shakily.

'Oh, yes, we do,' Piers corrected her.

'Like what?' she demanded.

'Like the fact that you have just made some very interesting comments about...about a certain matter... Have you *any* idea how jealous I was when I thought that Ben meant more to you than I did...when I thought you were defending *him*, protecting *him* from me?'

'You were jealous of *Ben*? But that's—' Georgia began weakly, but Piers interrupted her before she could finish speaking.

He said softly, 'That's very predictable behaviour for a man so desperately in love.'

'You...desperately in love...with me?' Georgia whispered. 'No, that's not possible.'

'You don't think so?' Piers asked her whimsically. 'Well, there are certain time-honoured ways of proving that it's true, but none of them I think are best witnessed by a third party—even a canine third party. Release, Ben,' he told the dog, who immediately released Georgia's arm and stepped back from her with a wag of his tail.

'I can't believe you've taught him so quickly,' Georgia said as Piers guided her along the hallway.

'Well, *I* can't take all the credit,' Piers told her. 'You had done all the groundwork, and I *have* been spending a lot of time with him since he's been here. After all, he's the closest thing I've got to you.

'How could you believe I'd go behind your back like that and get rid of him?' he asked her as he opened one of the doors off the hallway and stood back for her to precede him into the sitting room that lay beyond it.

'I don't know,' Georgia admitted honestly. 'I think I was just hurting so much from loving you... Piers,' she protested as he suddenly pushed the door shut with an audible bang and pulled her into his arms.

'Piers what?' he challenged her thickly, holding her so close to his body that she could feel the fierce, fast drumbeat of his heart. 'These last few weeks without you have been...' He stopped and shook his head, as though unable to find the words to describe his pain.

'And for me too,' Georgia agreed shyly. 'But if you love me,' she asked him, 'then why didn't you say so...when...?' She paused, drawing a very careful little design on his shirt-front with her fingernail, unable to look into his eyes just in case she had got it wrong after all and this was simply a cruel joke he was playing on her, a punishment he was inflicting on her.

'I tried to,' Piers told her simply. 'But every time I did you seemed to want to change the subject, and I thought it was because you didn't share my feelings.'

'No. *I* thought you were going to warn me off, to tell me that it was just sex, and say that I mustn't fall in love with you. *That's* why I stopped you. I knew it was already too late for me! I wouldn't have done the things I did...been so...so intimate with you if I hadn't loved you,' she told him, pink-cheeked. 'It's not... I'm not...'

'No, I did wonder about that,' Piers agreed. 'But to my mind there's no shame for a woman in physically wanting a man without being able to love him.'

'So you thought I felt lust and not love?' she asked him ruefully. 'What would we have done if I hadn't come round here today?' she added shakily. 'We could have—'

'No.' He stopped her. 'No. I hadn't given up... I've taught Ben to limp. It would have taken a good many visits to the surgery before you cottoned on to the fact that there was nothing wrong with his paw—or so I hoped!'

'Oh, Piers,' Georgia laughed. 'You *wouldn't* have...'

'Don't bank on it. The way I feel about you is—'

'Mmm...?' Georgia interrupted him, an invitingly husky note in her voice as she looped her arms around his neck and lifted her face towards him. 'The way you feel about me is...?'

Human beings did the oddest things, Ben reflected. His two were still upstairs in bed despite the fact that he should have had his dinner two hours ago, and not even a discreet bark outside the bedroom door had alerted them to their negligence... Never mind, there *were* home-made sausages in the fridge...!

He photographis like a pro) As all your ex-
bonus offered (incoherent mumbling for as while we go on
laughing out) I couldn't have a miskato put him to bed
hote.

'Morat… but I think he's not so curse gives you

EPILOGUE

'OH, JUST look at the dog; isn't he gorgeous…?'

Ben wriggled appreciatively as he heard the on-looker's praise. Personally he thought it a little undig-nified, a little infra dig, so to speak, to be carrying a basket of flowers, but *they* had insisted. They had even made him carry one up and down the driveway for weeks on end, just to make sure he knew what he was doing.

A basket of flowers…and here they were now, com-ing out of the church with everyone throwing rose petals at them.

Obligingly Ben went over to have his photograph taken with the bride and groom and their families…still carefully carrying his basket.

'Ben did marvellously well with the flowers, didn't he?' Georgia sighed happily to her new husband as the wed-ding car pulled away from the church.

'He did indeed,' Piers agreed.

'You're so clever to teach him to carry the basket,' Georgia giggled.

'Mmm… I think he got more oohs and aahs than we did,' Piers said wryly, 'which isn't very fair when you think that this is *our* special big day. He had his last month, when he was presented with his Brave Dog of the Year award.'

Georgia laughed reminiscently.

'He certainly enjoyed that, didn't he? He posed for

the photographs like a real pro. I'm glad your god-mother offered to look after him for us whilst we're on honeymoon; I wouldn't have wanted to put him in kennels.'

'Mmm... Let's hope the colonel's cat shares your feelings. Marmalade is rather elderly, and Ben, as you keep reminding me, is still a young dog. Now what does *that* look mean?' Piers quizzed her as he saw the soft, dreamy look darkening his new wife's eyes.

'I was just thinking that in a year or so's time Ben is going to be the perfect age to be around babies...'

'Babies?' Piers leaned closer to her. 'I see! Are we talking, I wonder, about *his* babies...or our own...?'

Laughter dimpled the smile Georgia gave him as she told him teasingly, 'Who knows? Maybe both.'

'Hmm... I see. Well, *we'd* better not waste any time, then, had we?' Piers murmured as he bent his head over and kissed her.

'Oh, I don't know...I don't mind if we have to practise a few times first,' Georgia told him blissfully as she snuggled into his arms.

As the wedding car pulled up at the hotel where they were to have their wedding reception, Piers told her softly, 'Oh, I thought we'd spent the last few months doing just that—and, so far as I'm concerned, no amount of practice can make things between us any more perfect than they are right now. I love you, Mrs Hathersage.'

'And I love you too,' Georgia whispered back.

In the back of Mrs Latham's Volvo Ben was happily demolishing the treat that the bridegroom had slipped him just before he'd got into the wedding car with his new bride.

Home-made sausages... Ben loved them—almost as much as handmade shoes... Mmm...!

Tyler Brides

It happened one weekend...

Quinn and Molly Spencer are delighted to accept three
bookings for their newly opened B&B, Breakfast Inn Bed,
located in America's favorite hometown, Tyler, Wisconsin.

But Gina Santori is anything but thrilled to discover her
best friend has tricked her into sharing a room with
the man who broke her heart eight years ago....

And Delia Mayhew can hardly believe that she's
gotten herself locked in the Breakfast Inn Bed
basement with the sexiest man in America.

Then there's Rebecca Salter. She's turned up at the
Inn in her wedding gown. Minus her groom.

*Come home to Tyler for three delightful novellas
by three of your favorite authors: Kristine Rolofson,
Heather MacAllister and Jacqueline Diamond.*

HARLEQUIN®
Makes any time special ™

Visit us at www.eHarlequin.com

CELEBRATE VALENTINE'S DAY WITH HARLEQUIN®'S LATEST TITLE—

Stolen Memories

Available in trade-size format, this collector's edition contains three full-length novels by *New York Times* bestselling authors Jayne Ann Krentz and Tess Gerritsen, along with national bestselling author Stella Cameron.

TEST OF TIME by Jayne Ann Krentz—
He married for the best reason.... She married for the only reason.... Did they stand a chance at making the only reason the real reason to share a lifetime?

THIEF OF HEARTS by Tess Gerritsen—
Their distrust of each other was only as strong as their desire. And Jordan began to fear that Diana was more than just a thief of hearts.

MOONTIDE by Stella Cameron—
For Andrew, Greer's return is a miracle. It had broken his heart to let her go. Now fate has brought them back together. And he won't lose her again...

Make this Valentine's Day one to remember!

Look for this exciting collector's edition
on sale January 2001 at your favorite retail outlet.

HARLEQUIN®
Makes any time special ™

Visit us at www.eHarlequin.com

PHSM

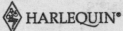

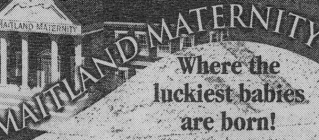

MAITLAND MATERNITY

Where the luckiest babies are born!

Join Harlequin® and Silhouette® for a special 12-book series about the world-renowned Maitland Maternity Clinic, owned and operated by the prominent Maitland family of Austin, Texas, where romances are born, secrets are revealed…and bundles of joy are delivered!

Look for

MAITLAND MATERNITY

titles at your favorite retail outlet, starting in August 2000

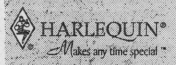

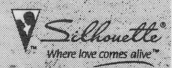

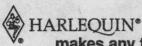

HARLEQUIN®
makes any time special—online...

eHARLEQUIN.com

your romantic
books

- 💜 Shop online! Visit Shop eHarlequin and discover a wide selection of new releases and classic favorites at great discounted prices.

- 💜 Read our daily and weekly Internet exclusive serials, and participate in our interactive novel in the reading room.

- 💜 Ever dreamed of being a writer? Enter your chapter for a chance to become a featured author in our Writing Round Robin novel.

• • • • • •

your romantic
life

- 💜 Check out our feature articles on dating, flirting and other important romance topics and get your daily love dose with tips on how to keep the romance alive every day.

• • • • • • •

your
community

- 💜 Have a Heart-to-Heart with other members about the latest books and meet your favorite authors.

- 💜 Discuss your romantic dilemma in the Tales from the Heart message board.

your romantic
escapes

- 💜 Learn what the stars have in store for you with our daily Passionscopes and weekly Erotiscopes.

- 💜 Get the latest scoop on your favorite royals in Royal Romance.

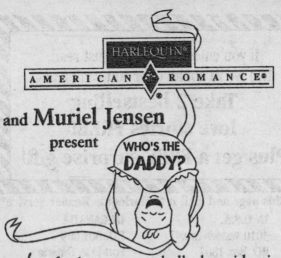